Betrayal of Peers

"Inception of the Hustle"

By: Calvin Haynes

Printed in the United States of America

Betrayal of Peers, A Novel Trilogy
ISBN: 9780988857100

First Edition

Address all inquires to:
Corporate Street Publication
PO BOX 682153
Houston, TX 77268

www.calvinhaynes.com

Logo Design: Timothy Washington
(a registered trademark of Corporate Street Publication)

Cover Design and Photography by: Lance Brown
Additional photography by: Kevin Williams and Garland Barefield

Dedications

I dedicate this street work of art, to the individuals that are labeled haters from all walks of life. Truly, the divine powers mysteriously sent some of you to exist within the realm of my presence. Ultimately causing some of the downfalls throughout my path in life. These experiences thus far have instilled profound proficiency within me. Being, that I am consciously aware of my purpose. I realize that the struggle has always been real and I meekly have all of you haters to be thankful for. This way of life has inspired me into pursing my most passionate interest….. Writing!

Betrayal of Peers

Prologue

This concept came to mind when I noticed a lot of people being unwillingly interrogated by law enforcement agencies. This particular game that I call cops and robbers has become somewhat an epidemic, in which the cops were winning. Ironically, because the robbers were now in cahoots with the enemy. I'm not siding with either entity; but simply expressing the robber's assiduous way of becoming so devoted in assisting the cops in a task they were employed to do themselves. Often this question reverberates in the mind: "Why bring somebody else down with you, when you are the one who made the blunder?" Maybe this is the noble thing to do, or maybe not. But as the axiom goes: A person that's old enough to understand his/her actions should be responsible for them. Without getting another party involved, if you know what I mean. As the old adage goes: what goes around, comes around. A type of karma that knows how to rear its ugly head. The protagonist in this literary work–whose name is Carlos Hudson, AKA, Cool – is about to realize what karma and betrayal are all about. Although Carlos has a couple of felonious charges under his belt, this still does not hinder him from partaking in any illicit activities when he hits the bricks, so to speak, even after doing a one year sentence in a low security state facility. This work of fiction is probably similar to a lot of characters of the world today. Perhaps it will even enlighten some of us to convert from the negative way in which we may live.

The setting takes place in Houston. In the neighborhoods of Sunnyside and South Park, on the southeast side of town. A place where mostly minorities live and the crime rate is stupendous. During the term of his incarceration, Carlos cultivated a hunger that would eventually lead him to wealth; as well as misfortune. His relationship with his first love has diminished immensely. His girlfriend, who was at his side for about eight years, decides to leave him hanging two months before he's released. This is due to his past infidelity and ongoing criminal activities. Reading his ex-girl's letter results in bitter pain. However, he recovers fast, due to the resilience he cultivated while incarcerated. A useful tool that would help him cope successfully in the free society. His plans now are to become fruitful – by any means necessary – upon his release. He will continue to be a product of his environment with the intentions and aim of totally becoming legitimate. His wealth increases along the way, even though he endures tribulations. He never imagined that outshining his peers would result in envy, but they just didn't seem to care much about their dreams and goals like he did. As long as the fast dough rolled in to squander on petty material goods – that allured the finest female hood rats – his counterparts were content. Not Carlos, even though he would lose focus from time to time. As most men do when their animal nature distracts them. This was a common problem he seemed to have experienced sporadically. What Carlos did not foresee in his forthcoming journey was the, "Betrayal of Peers."

Calvin Haynes

Chapter – 1

It's chow time at the Hilltop State Institution Trustee Camp, and Carlos Hudson, aka "Cool" decides not to attend. Instead, he chilled in his cubicle reading a novel by Donald Goines entitled; "Street Player". To him this book is therapeutic, as well as essential to his endeavors upon his release. He's been locked up for nine months already, with only three left to go. Therefore, it's important for his game to be tight. You see, while most of the other inmates sat around playing bones - as well as themselves - Cool was the type that was trying to get ready for free society. Focusing on his mind, body, and soul was a daily ritual for him, after he had finished slaving for the people in charge. When he first hit the camp, it was good to know that a few partners was down with him on the inside. Deep down he knew he wasn't going to be associating with too many inmates, because most were knuckle heads anyway. Cool vowed to himself that he'd never try to find one that wished to remain lost. Sometimes he goes against his convictions, lending a brother a hand, since he has the heart of a lion. Meaning his conscience wouldn't allow him to turn his back on fools. Although sometimes they might deserve to get shunned, he wouldn't belittle himself by stooping to another's level. Giving every individual the benefit of the doubt mostly; but if you messed over him, he would mess over you twice for disrespecting a real "G". While lounging in his cubicle one of his ace-boon-coons strolled up.

"What's up dawg, you ain't goin' to chow?" Blue asked. He got his moniker for having such a dark complexion.

"Naw man, I ain't goin', besides they ain't havin' nothin' but some swine anyway and I'm tired of that shit." Cool sighed, "We can hook up some roast beef later, ya dig?" he continued on with a Texas twang in his voice.

"I'm game my niggah, but I'm still gon' catch chow," Blue chuckled. "You still readin' that book fool?"

"Damn right! It's getting to the good part. This niggah stumbled up on a down bitch," Cool emphasized.

"I feel ya... I already know what's on ya mind fool," Blue leered.

"Yes suh, ain't no question. It's all about stackin' a dollar when I blow this joint. I ain't lettin' a few months ruin my hustle, ya dig?"

"I dig baby boy. So ya thinkin bout branchin' out into the pimpin' field, huh?"

"Let's jus' say I plan to broaden my horizons and diversify my portfolio." They both fell out laughing at Cool's axiom, until a C.O. (Correctional Officer) stole their attention.

"Mail call!" the C.O. announced.

"I'ma holla back at cha when I come from chow fool," Blue informed.

"Ah'ight baby boy, I'ma see if I got some fan mail. My broad ain't wrote me in a minute, that shit ain't normal kinfolk. I don't know what's wrong with that bitch," Cool flustered.

"Everythang probably straight dawg," Blue expressed.

"I hope so," Cool sighed.

"Let me know if he call my name kinfolk, I'll be back." They both headed toward the front of the dorm. Cool stood among the other inmates anticipating a letter like the rest of them. Another one of his partners emerged, just getting off of work – unkempt at best.

"What's up Cool," D.J. greeted.

"What's crackin' D," Cool replied; giving him some dap. "It's your world I'm just a squirrel tryna' get a couple of nuts, ya dig?"

"You know you the man," D.J. quipped. "Look out dawg."

"What up though," Cool replied.

"I'ma go wash some of this dirt off my blackass, let me know if a niggah got a kite," D.J. said; giving him dap as he strolled off.

"Yeah, you need to, I can smell ya stankin' ass," Cool bantered.

"Look out man!" D.J. turned around, pausing in his tracks.

"What's up?" Cool chuckled.

"Know what this mean?!" D.J. shot the middle finger, as he strolled off smiling.

"The same to you niggah!" Cool grinned. "I know the truth hurts, don't it?!" He shouted as everybody gazed at him. "You and Blue think I'm some kind of messenger! Y'all both askin' me to do the same shit! I'ma start chargin' you fools for my services!"

The C.O. bickered about Cool being disruptive during mail call, in which he respectfully subsided. He could hear D.J. laughing at him in the distance.

His last homeboy named Woog snuck up from behind with a mirthful expression on his face; tapping him on his shoulder. Just as Woog was about to tease him for getting scolded, the C.O. called Cool's name for mail. After Cool picked up his letter, he walked back over toward Woog.

"What's up man, you gon' let that C.O. talk to you like that?"

"I'm in hear for being a knucklehead, ya dig?" Cool shot back.

"Already," Woog agreed.

"Damn kinfolk!" Cool observed Woog's filthy body. "Them folks workin' the shit outta you, huh?"

"No doubt everybody ain't able to a have a Cadillac gig like you Cool baby, walkin' round here starched up lookin' all debonair," Woog signified.

"Yeah…But you know I had to pay dues first niggah"

"Already," Woog deferred. "Who wrote you?"

"It's my gal fool. I was just wonderin' when the hoe was gon' respond," Cool continued, "I'ma scream at you boys after I get through reading my kite. You gon' be ready to workout later on?"

"I guess if I feel up to it, they made a niggah weed eater the whole compound across the way," Woog sighed.

"Diz-zam! You can handle it though, you still a youngsta," Cool smirked.

"Whatever, niggah. I'll be at the crib," Woog replied; walking toward his cubicle.

As Cool strolled off, he reminisced about the days when he worked in the heat. The shit was no joke, he thought. Now D.J. and Woog still had to cope with the heat waves. The camp's location in East Texas didn't make weather conditions any better either. It got extra hot in the summertime and extra cold in the winter and it was now the last days of June. Cool and Blue worked on the inside as dorm orderlies. They both stayed crisp and clean, heat free. Regardless they had a job to do, minus the pay. The system still has its ways of evolving the slavery situation; oppression without monetary compensation. Finally making it to his cubicle, Cool tore open his letter vigorously. His psyche warmed him with a snafu vibe as to what he was about to read. He wasn't stunned when his girlfriend of eight years wrote the disappointing letter. He just wish she would have waited until he got out to explain to him face to face. He read it with a look of disgust on his face:

Dear Carlos,

I know it's been a while since I've wrote. I hope this letter finds you in the best of health. I'm okay just a little melancholy for what I'm about to say. Your cousin Red got killed the other day. I don't know exactly what happened, but I heard it was one of his so call homeboys who did it. Also, I've been dating this guy and I want to end our relationship, because I love him. I really don't think you're going to change, at least you haven't proven it to me. So I'm going on with my life and I hope you understand and respect my decision. I wish you all the best.

Sincerely,
Trina

Cool's heart shattered. He pondered if she ever loved him in the first place. But knew that wasn't the case. He had taken her through a little agony. As for his menacing cousin, he wasn't surprised. You live by the gun, you die by the gun, he thought. Red's mother, girlfriend, and son were surely to be burdened by his sudden death. Cool vowed to do what he could for them once he was released. The decision that his girlfriend made clearly affected his daily routine. Even his homies noticed. When they questioned his oddity, he would simply lie, stating everything was straight. Therefore, they would let him be. His eccentricity went on for about five days – until his resilience brought him back to normal. He resumed his daily routine, remaining humble like nothing ever happened. Since Trina's departure, he vowed never to let another woman break his heart again. Gradually, he was becoming a misogynist. Only he opts not to, because he has too much love in his heart to hate. So the next best thing was to add pimping to his resume´. Hell why not, he thought? Reading all the Donald Goines and IceBerg Slim books were inspiring. Besides that, he was a man adept at manipulation. The pimp game was always buried within his DNA, he just never utilized it. He decided from this point on – when he hit the bricks – that pandering would become secondary in his life. Although, his primary love was still for the drug trade. During these trying times, it now seemed that being incarcerated, along with his ex-girl's departure from his life, was a double dose of medicine that was only going to make him stronger and wiser.

CS

While Cool, Blue and Woog chilled in the day room, watching a rap video on BET, D.J. approached dancing without rhythm to the beat.

"What's up my niggahs," D.J. greeted.

"What up fool," Blue chuckled, laughing at his two left feet.

"What's going down," Woog added; chuckling also.

"Nothin' but the free world baby," D.J. boasted.

"Oh," Cool blurted; giving D.J. dap, "you bout to go to the crib ina minute, huh?"

"No doubt!" D.J. shot back.

"Don't forget to write ya digits down, 'cause you know a nig' like me be comin' right behind you," Cool insisted.

"How many months ya got left?" D.J. asked.

"Anotha three my niggah, an' I got somethin' in store for ya, if you true to this," Cool questioned.

"That goes without sayin', just hit me when you touch down," D.J. replied.

"D you gon' be ready?" Woog intervened.

"I was born ready," D.J. frowned.

"Okay niggah…I don't wanna see your ass back here," Woog sneered.

"Hell naw! They gon' have to drag my black ass back in a body bag!" D.J. retorted.

"Don't think they won't do it," Blue assured. They laughed at his remark, as they continued watching rap videos.

CS

A couple of days went by, and the C.O. announced ATW along with D.J.'s real name. Even though it was 5:00 AM, inmates were up at D.J.'s cubicle wishing him the best, exchanging addresses and phone numbers.

"Doug Johnson you want to stay here and socialize, or do you want to take your ass home?!" the C.O. bellowed in the distance.

"Gon' get outta here man, that sucka hatin," Cool warned.

"Fuck him! I'm on my way out the door!" D.J. snapped.

"Gon' get outta here dawg, before they make you play the waitin' game." Blue concurred; giving him a brotherly hug.

"No Shit…Ah'ight baby, until we meet again," Woog added; giving D.J. a hug also.

"I want a kiss when you come my way niggah," Cool joked, poking his lips out. D.J. walked towards him obligingly grinning with his lips poked out, while everybody who witnessed the comedy gazed in amusement. "I was just bullshittin' niggah," he continued menacingly; giving his homie a hug too. It's always good to see somebody leave this hell hole. But when someone leaves that's close, it always affects you emotionally for a minute, Cool conceded once D.J. had vamoosed.

CS

After D.J. left, it seemed like Cool's last few months flew by. Blue had another year left and Woog had almost two to go. Nevertheless, they were content. Considering the fictitious jurisdiction of the law they resided under, they knew matters could've been worst. D.J. never dropped a kite as he promised. This did not bother anyone but Cool. He was always sentimental towards a man's word. Partaking in one of their pastimes they congregated in the day room watching the tube.

"Well my niggahs tomorrow is the day," Cool began, "so let's have a fiesta… I got a couple cans of roast beef on it." They all nodded in agreement.

"I got the noodles and a couple cans of chili," Blue added.

"Y'all got that, I got the rest of the recipe dawg…What else is needed my niggahs?" Woog asked.

"Woog baby," Cool continued, "brang some tortillas, hot sauce, cheese, and whatever else you got to mix in the gumbo, it's a celebration, ya niggah goin' to the free world, ya dig?" Woog laughed, giving his homeboy dap. "Where the trees Blue?" as he switched topics with a whisper.

"Ain't got none, but I'll find some if y'all wanna blow," Blue chuckled.

"Damn right! This will be the last time I'ma kick it wit' y'all, for a minute!" Cool informed.

They all went to gather up the groceries for the spread and brought them to the back of the day room for preparation. Inmates passed by with greedy looks, envious of the three man shindig that was about to take place. A brother, who goes by the moniker Slim, walked up intervening.

"What's up people?" Slim continued. "You niggahs doin' the damn thang right, huh?" He gave them all dap.

"Ain't no question," Blue continued, "Say fool, you got some trees? Our boy leavin' in the mornin'," he asked Slim.

"Oh Shit! Cool ya outta here?!" Slim asked jovially.

"Fa Sho', blow a goin' away one wit' me bro'," Cool uttered in cadence

"I think I can come up wit' a lil' som'thin-som'thin', be back in a jif'," Slim said; strolling off to accommodate their request.

The cuisine was almost ready. Woog and Blue were putting the finishing touches on their jailhouse gourmet meal.

"Damn! I'm as good as Chef-Boy-R-Dee," Blue bragged; sampling the product.

"Niggah I don't get no credit, I help put it down too!" Woog snapped.

"Yeah, but I detailed it all homie," Blue replied.

"Fuck that dawg!" Cool interrupted. "While y'all argue I'ma dig in."

"Bless the food first o'hungry ass niggah!" Woog grimaced.

"You sure right dawg, my bad," Cool agreed.

They all held hands blessing the food gracefully. Just as they were about to dig in, Slim strolled back up with the cheeba.

"Here ya go baby boy," Slim said; handing Cool a joint.

"'Preciate ya, hold on to it, I'ma get my grub on first," Cool continued, "dig in kinfolk, make you a sammich."

"Don't mind if I do Cool baby," replied Slim. They all gathered around silently enjoying the food. Breaking the silence, Slim asked Cool a question that seemed redundant. "Look out Cool, I know you gon' handle up when you raise?" he asked curiously.

The fellas all chuckled knowing if Slim was really a member of the faction, he would already know the answer to his inane question. Slim had no idea of the type of prolific and ambitious perceptions Cool possessed. Cool looked over Slim's primitive characteristics, before reciting a quote from one of the many books he had read.

"Well Slim, let's just say durin' the duration of my incarceration, I armed myself with the necessary qualifications to function in free society, beyond the prison walls," Cool theorized; as they all chuckled giving each other dap.

"I see why they call you Cool," Slim inclined, "you a fly mu'fucka man."

"Yeah, I suppose you're right, it's a befittin' moniker," Cool boasted. "other niggahs use it, but don't represent it right, know-wha'- I'm-talkin'-'bout?"

After they all finished stuffing their faces, they went out on the yard to blow the joint; while continuing the chatter. Cool of course was the highly acclaimed storyteller, who always used cuss words in his diction, when explaining or expressing his thoughts. He truly wanted to be an entrepreneurial mogul; as well as see his cohorts excel along with him.

This was his odyssey. Feeling like he had to do dirt first. They stayed out shooting the shit until rack time. Cool was looking forward to the moment anyway; knowing this was his last day of dealing with the jail's babysitters. And hopefully I won't have to pay another visit in the future, he thought.

They all said their goodbyes to Slim, since he lived in another dorm. Then, they strolled to their own confined quarters.

"I want y'all to know before I bounce dawg, that I ain't gon' leave y'all hanging like that niggah D.," Cool sincerely announced, as he continued, "I'ma shoot a few flicks and a little change. Don't expect it every month though, ah'ight?"

They all chuckled knowing how real his statement was.

"It's all gravy," Woog said, "ya know how a niggah forget about you once he make it to the free world."

"That's right," Blue added.

"Dig that, but we 'pose to be down like four flat tires, tight like hallways, smoked out all day, ya dig?" Cool quipped; as they grinned at his fly vernacular. "Shit, I don't forget about my peeps, I guess them niggahs from Beaumont funny-style...I'm a check his ass when I get out, see where his head really at."

"I feel ya dawg," Woog uttered.

"That's right." Blue reiterated.

They were all from different cities in the same state. Cool was from Houston, Blue was from Columbus, Woog was from Amarillo, and D.J. was from the city of Beaumont, Texas. As they approached the dorm's entrance, Cool decided to do something zany. The C.O. that worked the late shift was a lush. Rumor had it that his thermos stayed full of crazy juice; i.e.- Vodka. Probably why he jabbered repetitiously all night about nothing.

"Look out my niggahs," Cool continued, "I'ma get a pen from this Mr. Furly lookin' ass C.O. when we go in here." They all chuckled. "We gon' exchange info. now, 'cause tomorrow I'm burnin' rubbah like the Gap Band. We all zooted, an' I know you boys gon' be tired then a mu'fucka in the mornin', so I'ma let you boys rest, kno-wha'-I'm-talkin'-'bout?"

"Yeah, that was some pretty good shit," Blue mumbled; eyes blood-shot red.

"Man," Woog snickered, "you ain't gotta fuck wit' that fool, I'll go get a pen out my locker."

"I know dawg, I jus' feel like harassing him before I bounce, hell, he always fuckin' wit' us for no reason," Cool smirked, while his homies smiled knowingly.

The C.O.'s name was Mr. Freddie, but Cool insisted on being cynical – evoking anger from the man by calling him out of his name – as they entered the dorm.

"Yo, what's upper Furly," Cool wise cracked; approaching the C.O.'s desk; while his homies gazed with amusement.

"Wha'….wha' what you call me inmate!" The C.O. stuttered irately.

"Man, let me borrow somethin' to write wit'. I ain't got time to bump wit cha, ya dig?" Cool continuously harassed.

Officers despised inmates who didn't address them in formal fashion. They were power stricken tyrants with the desire to crush an inmate's spirit anyway they could.

"I'm not your man," Mr. Freddie continued babbling, wha'...what's yo' your num...nu. number inmate, so I can wr...write your ass up!" Woog and Blue laughed at the frustrated C.O., while Cool maintained his composure, displaying a fractious mug. "C...c'mom, give it to me now!"

"Okay sucka I'll get a pen elsewhere then," Cool sneered; as he and his homies strolled off cackling at the theatrics.

"Yooou come back here Hudson, I'm n...not playing around!" Mr. Freddie fumed, the hue of his skin red as an apple.

"I'll catch you boys later before I go to sleep, an we'll exchange info. Let me see what this dickhead want," Cool chuckled; as the homies said all right in unison. They strolled off laughing at Cool's antics knowing he would get away with his foolishness.

The C.O. belligerently cursed Cool out with a volume that disturbed the entire dorm. He made a futile attempt to write Cool a minor case because he wanted him to do some extra duty hours of labor. Cool continued to act like an imbecile by refusing to sign the documents. The C.O. was so peeved he phoned the Sarge. Once the Sarge arrived he even had to laugh at Cool's shenanigans; knowing he was going home in the morning. Actually, damn near everybody knew; except the melon head, shit for brains, C.O. After the side show subsided, Cool strolled to both his partner cubicles;

exchanged information, distributed his property amongst them, gave them brotherly hugs, and went laid in his bunk until his name was called A.T.W.; all the way home.

Chapter – 2

It's a beautiful day in the neighborhood, so Black decides to get off his ass, and start the day off right. It's been awhile since he got up this early, but today was a special occasion. His main man was hitting the bricks. So, he had to get ready for such a glorious event. Black has a wife and kids. Still he's a man with quite a few paramours, awaiting his every beck and call to accommodate his lustful nature. Since his financial situation was on point, tricking was now one of his favorite hobbies. He has a small pest control business. But, his real finances come from the dope game. He shows little interest in his legit venture; letting his man Ray wield it. Ray holds it down until he is diverted into one of his infamous drinking binges, too impaired to handle his responsibilities. That's the only time Black will lend a hand. Most of the time, Black likes to hang out in the various titty bars throughout the city with his other homie Money – another freak monger.

Getting out of the shower, Black stepped to his mini bar making himself a Hennessy on the rocks, aware of the queasy feeling he might endure from not eating first. As he lounged sipping his drink, he phoned Ray to make sure he was handling his work ethics. Before Black hung up, he reminded Ray of the coming home party. Then, he phoned Money, praying to God that his employee was sober enough to do his daily duties. The phone rung several times before a fatigue voice on the other end grumbled incoherently.

"Money! Money!" Black screamed.

"Niggah," Money breathed heavily, "it's too fuckin' early dawg."

"Man get your crusty ass up, our niggah touch down today fool!" Black informed.

"No Shit?" Money said, with clarity in his voice now. "I can't wait to see him man. Wait til he get a load of us. How long that niggah been gone?"

"He got locked down in ninety-one, sooo, it's been' bout a year," Black replied dubiously," get ya ass in gear dawg, after I rendezvous wit' this dude about my new crib, we gon' go get e'erythang ready for my niggah comin' home party. Matter-of-fact, I'ma make reservations for the Presidential Suite at the Ritz Carlton. I hope it's not reserved, I want my boy to see how we roll now." Black phone line beeped. "Hol' on dawg let me see who this is," said Black.

"Ah'ight." Money replied.

"Hello," Black greeted.

"Is this Mr. Brown?" the gentleman asked properly.

"Yes it is, how may I help you," Black replied knowingly.

"How are you sir, it's your realtor Don Prichard," the agent assured.

"Ah yes, I'm fine. An' yourself?" Black asked cordially.

"Splendid sir. I was calling to see if you had time to meet me at the property site instead of my office?" Don asked.

"I don't see why not," Black frowned, "Is there a problem?"

"No sir," Don assured. "It's just that the construction of your home is almost complete, and I want to see if you are satisfied with the color of the marble tile before the guys lay it."

"Oh I see. I could make it there at eleven," Black continued, "it's 9:30 now. Will that be okay?" He glanced at his watch.

"That'll be fine sir," Don continued, "and I'll bring your keys, as well as the paperwork you need to sign."

"That'll be great. Thank you sir."

"No problem, it's my pleasure. Enjoy your new home and tell the wife and those beautiful little girls I said hello," Don responded with care.

"Okay good day to you Mr. Prichard," Black signed off; clicking back over to Money.

"Damn Man!" Money peeved. "All ya had to do was call me back dawg. Leave a nig' on hold for an hour!"

"My bad playboy it was my realtor," Black apologized.

"What he say?" Money asked curiously.

"He said my shit almost ready. We gon' meet at the property to confirm some mo' shit...Check it, I'ma get dress'd and slide through, you can roll over there wit' me. Then we can proceed with our original plan," Black implied.

"I know you can't wait to get away from them haters in the hood dawg," Money said.

"It's all good in the hood dawg, but I do need to escape the drama out here from time to time. I think e'ery niggah need a rest haven... hell," Black imagined.

"Dig that," Money continued, "say B., I got some scrilla for you too I..."Black cut him short.

"Chill baby boy, we'll discuss when I arrive. We don't need the world in our biz, ya dig?"

"My bad. I be forgettin' 'bout the line sometime," Money commented remorsefully.

"In a minute fool," Black chuckled.

"Already," Money snickered, as he hung up.

Talking on the phone is not the wise thing to do in their illicit profession. Black is the sort of boss that stays on top of his game; by taking proper precautions and staying away from petty dealers who sell crumbs. Dealing with a couple of people deems befitting enough for him. That's why he only dealt with Money and Cool – for the most part. Cool being his top soldier of course. But Money was his alternative until his main man hit the bricks. Money understood this, besides, if it wasn't for Cool's convincing rhetoric, Money probably wouldn't have come thus far. Bringing Money into the crew while Cool did his bid, turned out to be the right thing to do.

One would have to give Black his props. He is a white collar street delegator who stays away from the streets, as much as possible. Simultaneously, supplying the illicit product he and his constituents reaped rewards from.

CS

Black cruised along in his Ford LTD hooptie damn near to his destination. His luxurious ride was an onyx black Infinity Q-45; with all the trimmings, eighteen inch; three piece chrome BBS wheels: Plus, a ten thousand dollar sound system. Being a smart hustler, he kept it in a secure storage garage. He didn't show off much, and he definitely didn't want the attention everyday. When he arrived at Money's crib, his man was lounging outside, Versace down, with alligator sandals on his feet. Sipping Moet and Alize' mixed; puffing on a blunt.

"What up kid?" Money uttered; approaching with a cup in one hand; Crown Royal bag in the other one; as well as a blunt between his lips.

"Damn dawg" Black chuckled. "You got a lot of shit goin' on. Hop yo' wild ass in fool!" Money laughed at his remark; dropping the blunt from his mouth.

"Damn! Hold this man," Money said; handing him the bag and cup while retrieving the blunt, and relighting it once he got inside the car.

"Let me hit it dawg," Black said surprisingly.

"So, you smokin' wit' me today, huh slick?" Money chuckled.

Black blew sporadically, but Money is a chain smoker.

"Might as well fool," Black continued, "today is a good day. How much in the bag?"

"About five stacks. What I owe eleven mo'?" Money questioned.

Black pulled out this organizer; which tallied his day to day activities.

"Let me check," Black said; reaching for the blunt; taking a hit while coughing from the high powered smoke.

"Take it easy dawg, Money smirked, "that ain't ya typical 'hood trees. I cop that from this white boy name Skull. Peckerwood said he was gon' have some mo' of that good Cali bud today."

"Shit N….." Black coughed continuously. "Niggah you tryna kill me?"

Money laughed boisterously. "I can't kill my dawg! You just can't inhale this type of shit like it's Reggie! This that seedless bionic chronic, know-wha'-I'm-talkin'-'bout?!" he exclaimed.

"Whatevah…. Here, take this shit," Black grimaced, "I'll stick to my liquor."

"I ain't mad at cha fool, mo' for me. Matter-of-fact, when you through runnin' ya errands, take me by Skull's place, to see if I can cop me anotha sack". Money announced.

"You know I ain't tryna' go to no hot spots. Where the Wood stay?" Black asked with a frown on his mug.

"By Almeda Mall. E'erythang straight o' scary ass niggah, I kno' not to put you in danger B", Money assured. "By the way, it's eleven five you owe niggah," Black continued scrolling through his organizer," you ain't forgot about the ol' five, huh?"

"Naw, but I thought you did," Money retorted honestly.

"Ha….!" Black screeched. "You know I love money!" he mimicked Frank White; on the "The King of New York" movie; while Money chuckled knowingly.

They made it to Black's new house a little earlier than arranged. Mr. Prichard hadn't arrived yet, so they decided to browse the premises.

"Where that cracka at? He's late." Money asked.

"Naw, I'm early, but let's have a look shall we? He should be pullin' up in a few," Black suggested, "the people that's workin' don't know me, but fuck'em."

"Say man, I'ma tell ya right now, judgin' from the exterior, yo' shit dope," Money praised.

"Thanks, now I got a place to park my up to date slab, instead of that high ass storage," Black replied.

They got out the car and went inside. The workers leered like they didn't belong, but never the less, continued their chores. The realtor finally showed up ten minutes late apologizing for his tardiness. Black signed the documents, while asking if his spouse or mom needed anything else. A little dubious of some of the procedures, because the property was in their names, not his. One of the golden rules a dope dealer must abide by: never put anything too exorbitant in your name, just in case the shit hit the fan.

"Once again congratulations, and call me if you need anything," Mr. Prichard assured.

"You're welcome," Black replied as they shook hands.

Black and Money contemplated Cool's release as they were leaving. "I'ma call Cool's T-Jones an' see if she know what time he'll be home dawg," Black said as they cruised along.

"Dig that," Money continued, "I'ma call some hoochies and make sure they be available for tonight's shindig."

They picked up their cell phones simultaneously. Money conversing with the girls while Black awaited an answer at the Hudson's residence.

"Hello Ms. Hudson, this is Black. How you doin'?" He greeted.

"I'm fine." Ms. Hudson replied with a chipper tone. "Who you lookin' for, Carlos?"

"Yes ma'am," Black continued, "I was wonderin' what time he'll be there?"

"Child I don't know" Ms. Hudson sighed, "it should be today, 'cause I received a call from them folks."

"I see. Well, have him give me a call. You still have my number, right?" Black asked.

"Sure, I have it." Ms. Hudson responded. "I'll let him know. Don't be gettin' my baby in no trouble, ya-hear?"

"No ma'am!" Black explained. "We jus' givin' him a comin' home party!" he chuckled.

As they were saying their goodbyes, Black was now pulling in the storage parking lot to exchange vehicles. Money continued to entertain the broads over the phone, while Black pondered about making Cool a fifty/fifty partner in his underground endeavors. He knew his main man had balls of steel, and would never snitch on his comrades. Iron clad trust like that, is hard to find in most street dealers these days.

Chapter – 3

C arlos was now on a Greyhound Bus heading to Houston, Texas. Gazing out the window, he noticed the massive face lift along the highway. Pondering the facts, made him realize his year stay was indeed, a blessing in disguise. Most people were in far worse conditions. Especially the ones who got caught with that crack. If one ever got nabbed, the powder cocaine was definitely the way to go. The system is designed to be nefarious toward the hard stuff. Considering the minority street dealers dealt mostly with that. An insidious way to bring down the less fortunate, Carlos thought. Heedless to the pitfalls of the game, he vowed from the first time he got paid underground juggling, that he would ball till he fall. But yet, be more productive and constructive this time around.

"What time is it?" Cool asked another released inmate sitting across from him.

"About 4:30," replied the stranger.

"How long will it be before we get downtown man?" Cool implied again.

"Within the next hour if the bus driver push this bitch," the stranger continued. "What's yo name dawg, and what set you from?"

He sounded like a gang banger. Looks can be deceiving, Cool thought. "I'm from the Park dawg, they call me Cool....Why what's up?" he sneered.

"I was just wonderin' homie, didn't mean no harm, he gave Cool dap as he continued, "I'm from fifth ward....I got some cousins out there in South Park, they stay off MLK. Y'all got them hoes out there dawg."

"They ah'ight, but a niggah want somethin' worthy, know-wha'-I'm-talkin'- `bout? I ain't trippin' on no skeezers," Cool smirked.

"Yeah I feel ya, but I been down five tight," the stranger sighed.

"No shit!" Cool grimaced.

"Yes sir. I'll damn near stick my dick in a hole in the ground, right about now, ya dig?" They both laughed at the stranger's cliché.

"You didn't even tell me ya name kinfolk?" Cool asked.

"Mark… Say Cool, maybe we can have a drink when we get downtown to celebrate our freedom," he suggested.

"Naw man, maybe some otha time, I got folks waitin' for me. Slide me ya digits, we can hookup later on though," Cool assured.

"I can dig it, I know baby probably waitin' on you," Mark assumed.

He wrote down his hookup and gave it to Cool. Afterwards, they rode in silence. Cool's intuition led him to believe dude was alright. Although, he heard how shady them fifth ward cats were. Who knows, Mark might turn out to be a prospect toward prosperity, he thought as he dozed off.

Chapter – 4

Black and Money were now cruising in luxury. Heading towards the liquor store to cop a baller's favorite elixir; Cristal champagne, and some bottles of Alize´ to concoct it. Along the way, Money reminded Black again to shoot by Skull's crib to cop the last sack of Cali bud, before they stopped by the Ritz Carlton to pay in person for the lavish suite. Everything was going according to plan. They rode along enjoying the banging sound system; ecstatic about the upcoming release of their homeboy.

"Look out Money!" Black began; grabbing the remote; turning down the volume so he could hear himself speak.

"What up?" replied Money; still bobbing his head to the beat.

"Them boppas said they were comin' huh?' Black asked.

"No doubt," Money continued, "I got a couple comin', I want my niggah to have both of 'em, It's been a while since he handled up, know-wha'-I'm-talkin'-'bout?" he chuckled.

"Who ya got comin' man?" Black smirked.

"Rio an' Porsche, them freaky bitches from Foxes," Money said with delight.

"Ah'ight," Black smiled deviously, "them bitches will do. I'ma get my bitch Roxanne to come, an' brang one mo' wit' her, so that fool can have four, know-wha'-I'm-talkin'-' bout?" They gave each other dap.

"Already, that niggah need to alleviate some of that tension, Money remarked, "Ya know man, them hoes be wantin a hundred fi'ty a piece just to show up."

"Can't knock the hustle dawg," Black continued, "this one on me," he said holding up the Crown Royal bag full of cash.

As they parked in the front of the hotel, Black got out leaving a bickering Money behind; while he went to go check in. He was peeved at Black for not stopping by Skull's house first. He wanted to score the last sack of sticky bud; knowing how unpredictable dope fiends were.

Back on the road again, Money's pager began to ring like a high school bell. He ignored all clientele, due to the festivities. Except for one cat who owed him money. He had learned a long time ago, that in the dope game once a consignment worker call you to pick up, it's necessary that you do so – simply because shit happens. He coerced Black to take him to pick up the ends. He complained, but chilled, because the cash was coming to him. Besides, Black pondered paying his debt early and copping a few more bricks from his superior. Being a made niggah has it's advantages. Meaning, he never needed the cash up front.

Since they purchased a substantial amount of beverages, Money popped open a couple of bottles; mixing them some thug passion to quench their thirst. Suddenly, Black's cellular phone rang stealing their attention.

"Hello," Black greeted.

"Wha'd up kinfolk!?" Cool shouted jovially.

"Who this?" Black feigned; knowing exactly who it was; detecting the voice.

"Gon' on wit' that shit dawg," Cool hissed, "you better recognize."

"Man who would you like to speak to?" Black continued the shenanigans; while Money leered dubiously.

"Niggah! This Cool mu' fuckin' C! How ya livin' baby?!" Cool bellowed frantically.

"Niggah I know who this is!" Black chuckled. "So you back in the place to be huh babyboy?!"

"No doubt! Where that damn Money at?!" Cool asked with alacrity.

"That fool right here. Wanna holla at him?!" Black asked. "Here man he wanna holla atcha", handing Money the phone.

"Wha'd up kid?!" Money said with glee.

"Back from hell G," Cool sighed, "in servitude like a fuckin' animal...Looks like shit done changed."

"Ain't no secret" Money stressed, "I'ma pull your coat to the actual factuals, know-wha'-I'm-talkin'-'bout?"

They conversed for thirty minutes, conceding they would be by to scoop him up after making a couple of runs. Then, they hung up.

Thirty minutes later, they were creeping down Brandon St. Ironically, Cool was coming out the house just as his homies were pulling up. As he strolled toward the car, his homie gaped at the physical physique he had cultivated on the inside.

"How are you Shannon...Michael?" Cool jeered formally.

Cool was being cynical; knowing his confidants despised their real names. Like most cats in the 'hood, they preferred using monikers. In case calamity occurred, nicknames made the authorities' task a little more difficult to find the suspects.

"Yo, hop your fly ass in dawg," Money smiled. Cool got in the back seat. "Get one of them cups back there, so I can pour you up some of this Thug Passion, I would blo' some of this killa wit' cha, but I know you can't fuck around yet."

"Niggah you on swoll. Been down there gettin' yo' paper huh?" Black added.

"No doubt, Cool responded "Yeah niggah, I could use some Thug Passion, whatever that is."

"What the hell was that I saw on your feet dawg?" Black grimaced; while Money chuckled.

"These them rhinos kinfolk, ya'll don't know nothin' 'bout that," Cool stressed, "especially you Black, niggah you ain't never seen the inside of a jailhouse." They all let out a boisterous laugh, as Money passed him his drink.

"Fuck you niggah!" Black sneered. "You ain't the only one that got game! I ain't never been, and don't ever plan on going!"

"I feel you babyboy," Cool agreed, as they laughed in an uproar.

"Anyway back to that bullshit on your feet," Black continued jokingly, "you can't be hangin' out wit' us niggah, sportin' them Paul Bunyans." They all laughed. "I'ma shoot by the mall; get cha somethin' tight, ah'ight?"

"You ain't made it there yet?" Cool retorted. "Y'all niggahs funny at best, laughin' at a niggah 'cause he ain't came up yet…Sympathize dawg, a nig' just raise, know-wha'-I'm-talkin'-'bout?"

"It's all good babyboy," Money chuckled, "we got a treat for you."

"I ain't trippin', I know I'm overdue for some love, understand me? But I'm ready to get my serve on, Cool sighed.

"Chill babyboy," Black emphasized, "you just raised, you got plenty of time to get busy, besides, you don't need to be poundin' the pavement so soon.

"I feel ya Black. I ain't in no rush, but I ain't tryna waste no time either... I'm ready to make 'em pay baby," Cool stressed seriously.

They laughed at his eager expression; knowing how much of a zealot he is when it boiled down to attaining street profitability. However, out of concern, the homies didn't want to see Cool fall prey to the system again. They figured since he got out, he didn't need to be going back next week.

CS

Inside the Galleria Mall, Cool was astounded by the immense amount of love shown by Black. For him to shell out a thousand dollars for a Gucci hook up from head to toe; as well as a pair of seven hundred dollar, gold frame, Cartier´ eyewear, Cool figured they must 've been ballin' harder than he imagined. All G'd up like his counterparts; they headed out to a destination not far from the mall, which was to be Cool's ultimate surprise: bonafide playa-style entertainment.

He didn't know what to expect when they pulled up at the palatial hotel. As they rode the elevator to the plush suite; located at the pinnacle of the hotel, Cool was in awe, taken a back by the space, as well as the amenities.

"Damn kinfolks! This the shit I been missin'?!" Cool announced, as they entered the lavish surroundings. "We left the champagne in the ride."

"It's all good," Black began pompously, "the bellboy will take care of it my niggah."

"Mus' be nice to live the high life," Cool expressed, as he flopped down on a sumptuous leather recliner.

Browsing the suite, Cool could definitely tell it was top notch. There was a giant jacuzzi, a baby grand piano, and a superb balcony with a panoramic view of Houston's skyline. Fifteen minutes later, a gentleman; with the aura of a royal courtier, brought the fellas the beverages that were in the car. They hob nobbed for a while, until another knock at the door grabbed their attention.

"Answer the door Cool," Money said, as he and Black smiled knowingly.

"Niggah why you can't answer it?! Cool joked. "I'm tryna relish the moment, know-wha'-I'm-talkin'-'bout?!"

"Niggah get the damn door!" Black demanded. "It's probably for you anyway!"

"Ah'ight dawg, since you put it that way," Cool smirked, "don't mind if I do."

He strolled toward the door skeptically ready for whatever. As he answered the door, three lovely looking females promenaded through, possessing some duffel bags and a boom box. They all smiled knowing the fiesta was about to go down. The females sashayed to one of the rooms to change, stepping back on the scene in their birthday suits.

Curiously, Black asked his girl Roxanne about the fourth hoochie that was supposed to be present. In which, she replied with a dumb-founded shrug. Nonetheless, the party still turned out to be a gyrating freakfest. The broads worked what they mama gave them. But the erotic dynamics didn't arouse Cool. The girls diligently tried to awaken his flaccid penis. They were some dime pieces too, but Cool had dead presidents on his mind. His big headed thoughts thwarted his little head's performance.

The broads cynically bickered, but he didn't care. Having knots in his pockets was far greater than pussy any day, he thought. After a few hours of lewd strip club style entertaining, the girls left. The homies analyzed Cool's oddity, and assumed he didn't have a good time – even though he did. His mind was just somewhere in the future, and the whole engagement caught him off guard.

"Before you niggahs start in on me," Cool smirked, "I want y'all to kno' a niggah wasn't skittish of them hoes."

"I can't tell niggah!" Black sneered. "Let me find out you done flopped!"

Money spat up some of his drink; laughing at Black's antics.

"You got me bent kinfolk!..It's all about the big faces, know-wha'-I'm-talkin'-'bout?! I got plenty of time to get my freak on!" Cool emphasized.

"Aw shit, here we go again," Black tittered, "you gon'get paid niggah, have some fun, you just raised."

Money nodded his head in agreement.

"I feel you man," Cool agreed, "but check it, a niggah can get some cunt, when he can't get nothing to eat. Don't get me wrong dawg, I appreciate the love. I'm jus'ready to catch in, 'cause if I try to catch up I'm bound to get fucked off again, ya dig?"

"I feel ya" Money admitted, "we just want what's best for you, that's all. We can't afford to lose you again my niggah."

Cool felt grateful for having such noble comrades concerned for his well being.

Since Money and Black were hitched, they both decided to leave Cool behind to finish relishing the lavish suite. As he walked them to the car, Black vowed to come back and pick him up early in the morning; while joking about the exorbitant bill he would incur if he kept the room another day.

CS

Pooped out from a hectic workday, Trina was now slipping on her pajamas. She damn near went to sleep while in the tub, until her Scottish terrier disrupted her. As she crawled into bed, the chatter of her phone caused her to whine in frustration. She opted not to ignore it, because she didn't want it disturbing her parents.

"Hello," Trina answered groggily. "Oh, hi Carlos…" "Shit boy I'm tired, I been on my feet all day…" "You think" He cut her off. "Look, now, I explained to you about how I felt…" "I'm not finna come up there, you know I got a boyfriend…" "We still friends, but my heart with someone else Carlos, furthermo', I'm tired, just call me back some otha time…" "I'm not actin' shitty, I don't need to come up there no way…" "We don't need to be alone…." "For what?" "Look, I gotta go…." "Well, I wish you all the best too…" She yawned. "Good night."

Unaware of her own impertinence she hung up, and fell to sleep instantly.

Laying in the bed feeling like a sucker, Cool wished he hadn't ignored his playa ethos. He felt like a simple nitwit for even picking up the phone and wasting his time. Not even his manipulative mouthpiece could change his obstinate ex-girlfriend's mind. She was as stubborn as a jackass, he thought. Mulling about all the fishes still in the sea, his resilience rebounded. Making him phone a broad named Renee´. She was a sexy little number that used to visit him sporadically while he was incarcerated. Delighted to hear from him, she rushed up to the hotel to avidly serve her pussy on a platter. When she arrived, she embraced him with hugs and kisses; causing his rod to get harder than a roll of quarters. It was indeed her voluptuous physique that made his rod jump for joy, he thought, as he led her to the bedroom. She brought the beast out of him – something the previous girls couldn't do. He pierced her cunt with agility; making her climax at least three times. Judging from the juices that spilled all over his man hood, and the numerous times she screamed in ecstasy, made him realize he was still a stud.

Afterwards, she snuggled under him; simultaneously drifting off in a coma like sleep. He thought it was ironic that his member didn't respond earlier to the so-called professionals; as he laid back reminiscing. A couple of hours elapsed. His libido was ready for round two. They copulated once again; fiercer than before. The second freak session lasted until morning. Since Renee´ had to go to work, she took a shower, and demanded him to call her later on for round three, before she headed off. After Cool let her out, he decided to get some shut-eye before Black showed up. He wanted to be fully rejuvenated, because he had people to see, places to go, and money to make.

Chapter − 5

Black snuck through the door around 11:00 AM trying to startle Cool. He had a notion his homie was still asleep. Use to people waking him, the scare tactic was in vain. Besides, where he just came from, one never knew when a fracas might jump off. Being a light sleeper was essential. Cool woke up cranky, bickering about the futile scare attempt.

"You can't scare me ol' black ass niggah, they had niggahs mo' uglier than you where I was, playa!" Cool bantered, yawning.

"Fuck you man!" Black smiled.

"Where Money at?" Cool asked.

"Still layin' on his ass, like you probably. I haven't talked to him," Black replied.

"Yeah I had Renee´ in here last night fool, I tried to break that bitch pelvic bone, know-wha'-I'm-talkin'-'bout?" Cool bragged.

"Em-hm," Black joked, "but you was actin' gay when them otha hoes was here." Cool shot the middle finger as he got out the bed.

"So what's on the agenda for today?" Cool asked.

"Get dressed, I'ma go check out and then we ride out to my niggah pad, I need to drop off some change," Black informed, as he guzzled down some of the left over champagne on the table.

"Dig that," Cool continued, "niggah I don't see how you drankin' that shit hot," he frowned.

"Fuck it, this the good stuff dawg," Black transposed. "I think you already know my niggah. Remember Big Jerry that used to hang 'round Vince back in the day?"

"Ya know I know fat ass," Cool grimaced.

"I forgot you probably served him before," Black said knowingly.

"No doubt," Cool continued, "So, he's who you got to take the change to?"

"Yep. Do you remember Batman?" Black asked.

"Yeah, that's that niggah who use to serve Vince before he got lock'd up, huh?"

"That's him" Black assured.

"What he been up to?" Cool asked curiously.

"Pushin' weight like a mu'fucka, in a major way, Black emphasized. "Well anyway, he supplies Jerry an' Jerry supplies me, and a couple mo' niggahs you'll soon meet."

"Sounds like some supa tight slick shit to me," Cool said.

"No doubt…Fuck it, I might as well wait on you now," Black glances at his Rolex as he continued, "I was gon' run down and checkout right quick…Hurry up my niggah befor these mu'fuckas get to trippin', it's almost check out time."

"Ah'ight, I'll be ready in a minute," Cool strolled toward the lavatory, as he continued, "jus' need to get rid of the dragon, know-wha'-I'm-talkin'-'bout? Look out Black!"

"Wha'd up?!" Black replied.

"How much this room set cha back dawg?!"

"You don't wanna know dawg! Might scare the shit outcha, if I tell you!" Black smirked; hearing his homie laughing in the distance.

"It cost that much kinfolk?!" Cool chuckled.

"Nineteen hun'ed! Woulda cost mo' than that if they didn't gimme a discount!" Black assured.

"You that niggah!" Cool exclaimed, as he stepped out putting on his apparel, "I'm almost ready my niggah...where the fuc'?" he mumbled; scouring the huge surroundings in search of his shoes. "Oh, I see 'em, he continued. "I'm ready now damn fool."

"Look out man," Black said; reaching in his pocket pulling out five crispy one hundred dollar bills, "a little som'thin-som'thin so you can have some change in your pocket.

"Good lookin' B," Cool accepted as he continued, "you can't keep breakin' me off like this."

"Ain't shit. You need to chill for at least anotha week. See what's happenin' befor you just jump out there," Black admonished.

"Dig that. I feel you. I know you want me to protect my neck, but I'm one of them independent niggahs, I ain't finna waste too much time, know-wha'-I'm-talkin'-'bout?"

"Ah'ight niggah," Black flustered; shaking his head intensely.

They were now outside getting in the car. It didn't take Black long to check out. He slid the valet attendant a twenty spot before they headed off to their destination.

"Good lookin' out on that room dawg," Cool beamed.

"You ain't seen nothin' yet niggah," Black smirked, as he continued, "I'ma rent you a car so you can have some wheels. That niggah Jerry 'pose to sell me one of the work cars like they roll in."

"So whatcha sayin', y'all niggahs done got high tech on me now?"

"Somethin' like that. They come equip wit' stash spots, instead of wildin' out like you used to, you can put that shit up in case five-o decides to harass you.

"Dig that. Drivin' especially being black can be a mu'fucka, Niggahs in the 'hood shoulda been had it where you could conceal that shit."

"Well, it ain't like stash spots are new wave, it's just that we on anotha level now and havin' one handy is inevitable... Niggah can't flee wit' a shit load of bricks." Black enlightened.

"Already! Well, since it's on an' poppin' like that, it's a done deal...I'll take your advice, and take a chill pill.. Scope out the environment for the usual suspects that I deem worthy," Cool transposed, "man we been rollin' for awhile now. Where the fuck that niggah stay in the suburbs?"

"Somethin' like that. The niggah got a spot up in Sugarland, we'll be there in fifteen mo' minutes," Black replied.

"So, Batman let Jerry take over?" Cool assumed.

"Something like that."

"That niggah Bat' been slangin' for awhile, it probably was best that he appointed hisself a CEO...I know he up to his ass in chips, and never got jammed either!" Cool shrieked with emphasis.

"Evil faces in all the right places," Black smirked, "you gon' trip when you see how we do. When you build your clientele back up I want us to become fi'ty/fi'ty partners."

"Already!" Cool responded jovially.

"Instead of payin' me for a kilo or two, we'll jus' combine our patrons and split the profit. You game?" Black asked seriously.

"Already! Ya know how long I been waitin' to hear some shit like this?! Too long," Cool said deliriously.

"While you out there recruitin', I want you to be on the lookout for a crib wit' a garage, somewhere on the outskirts of the hood. Get one of your skeezas, that's straight, to put it in her name. We need a new place to keep the shit, an' you need a place to lay ya head. Kill two birds wit' one stone," Black informed.

"I ain't trippin', ya kno I'm 'bout it," Cool said with surety. "I'll look out for you, til you get on your feet. We can go half on the hooptie if Jerry fat ass ever get it to us. I've been askin' that fat fuck about that damn car way before you got out," Black scoffed, as he continued, "it's a hand me down, but it got a tight stash in it. He suggested not to use it for highway purposes, but it's all good in the 'hood though."

Cool listened attentively to Black's prospering rhetoric, realizing now that the time had finally come for him to shine.

As they finally arrived at Jerry's home, Cool was sublimed by the beauty, as well as the square footage of the mini mansion. Since Jerry was the protégé to the head of the faction, Cool pondered just how opulent the HNIC's (Head Niggah in Charge) homestead was.

"Get out man," Black insisted; taking Cool out of his reverie, "I told him I was brangin' you, that niggah know what time it is." As they got out a bald head cat greeted them. Black handed the eerie looking dude a black leather bag he retrieved from the trunk, as he continued. "Wha'd up Jim? This my niggah Cool, he jus' got out the joint…Where's that fat fucka?"

"He in there," Jim chuckled, "welcome home Cool. How ya doin'? He asked cordially; giving him dap.

"E'erythang-e'erythang kinfolk, just glad to be back, ya-feel-me?" Cool sighed grinningly.

"Dig that," Jim chuckled, "I'ma run upstairs and let him know y'all here y'all make ya-selves at home. He probably still layin' on his ass."

Jim is one of Jerry's street employees. He handled deliveries, as well as security – for the most part. Peeping the format, Cool sensed he was about to become a factor of a well-heeled establishment. Jerry came wallowing downstairs in his boxer underwear exposing his full rotund figure; with morning matter still in his eyes.

"Damn o' black ass niggah!" Jerry bickered. "I didn't think your ass was comin' this early!"

"It's time for you to get yo' Sam sausage head ass up! Fuc' you gon' do, sleep the day away?!" Black joshed, as they all laughed at him.

"I got it like that niggah, if I want to sleep for a year it's all gravy," Jerry bragged, as he continued, "I been up all night fuckin' wit' Hank and Junior trickin' asses. Black you miss'd it, we had some freaks outta Centerfolds…Ya know the shake joint off Richmond?"

"I know where Centerfolds at niggah," Black grimaced.

"I forgot, you trick harder than them niggahs," Jerry retorted, as everybody burst out laughing.

"I know you didn't, niggah!" Black shot back. "You the grand daddy of trickin'! I betcha all yo' bitches got rides, compliments of yo' fat ass!"

Everybody broke out in hysterical laughter at his remark.

"Aww, fuck you niggah!" Jerry giggled, as he continued. "At leas' I ain't alone in my trickin' endeavors.

Besides, niggah, if I wanted to buy 'em a crib to go wit' it, I'm like that, know-wha'-I'm-talkin'-'bout?"

"Whaatevah, niggah, I don't give a fuck, long as you keep me supplied," Black hissed, as he continued. "You remember Cool, huh?"

"You know I remember him. What's up man, ready to get rich?"

Cool chuckled at his haughty persona. He paused reminiscing of the days when he used to serve Jerry a few ounces from time to time, before he replied.

"No doubt, " Cool began, "I see you done came up, las'time I saw you, you was scorin' the shit from me."

"Yeah. Now the tables done turned niggah, you get to work for me now," Jerry retorted.

"Naw, niggah, I work for myself, kno-wha'-I'm-talkin'-'bout? Cool corrected, as he continued. "You just supply the shit we all benefit."

"You sure right, that's why if your li'l ass get caught, be sure to tell five-o the same shit!" Jerry insulted.

They all chuckled at his genuine gesture.

"Shh," Cool hissed, "you ain't got to worry 'bout that dawg, I'm as real as they come, snitchin' ain't even in my vocab', know-wha'-I'm-talkin'-'bout?"

"How much you brang Big Poppa," Jerry said; diverting his attention back on Black.

"Nifty fifty, I owe you thirty mo'," Black confirmed with a fly vernacular. "So when the hoop' gon' be ready? Ain't no need in takin' these constant risk, my niggah just raised, and he ready to work. I don't wanna have him out there bad."

"I feel ya" Jerry agreed, "y'all niggahs need to get a crib too, so my peeps can stop comin' through hot ass Southpark with that shit."

"We workin' on that Tiny," Black joked, as they chuckled. "But for now we need the wheels."

"I'ma have Jim drop it off to y'all later on wit' some mo'shit if you need it," Jerry hinted.

"Fuck it, brang five mo'," Black urged.

"I need to get rid of some mo' of this shit anyway… And give me at leas' half down on the car too niggah," Jerry reminded.

"You ain't gon' do nothin' but trick it off," Black signified, "I'll be back at the crib after I go get this niggah a rental."

"It'll be a minute anyway, Jim got to get the car from Hank's crib. Now ya'll get out my damn house, I'm finna go back to bed."

"Fat lazy fuck!" Black fumed, as they laughed.

"I'll be all that," Jerry continued, "jus' go make my scrilla ol' charbroil ass niggah!" he jived; as they cracked up off of his antics.

Jim assured he would be by later with the hooptie and illicit goods before Black and Cool headed off to go complete their mission.

As they rode on their way to the rental car agency, Cool began to criticize Jerry's arrogant demeanor.

"That's a cocky fat bastard," Cool smirked,"niggah get a li'l paper under his belt, an' don't know how to act, huh?"

"He ah'ight, but I can't front, he a messy mu'fucka," Black chuckled, as he continued, "fat ass got it goin' on, though. Niggah got a soul food restaurant and a record company."

"That's good, at leas' the niggah doin' somthin' wit' his paper, instead of squanderin' it like most cats."

"Don't think that fat fucka don't be fuckin' off, he like to gamble and trick too much. That fool fuck off mo' in a month than mos' mu'fuckas wit' a good gig make in year.

"Damn! I hope the niggah well stacked, fuc' aroun' and wind up a destitute." They both chuckled at Cool's statement as he continued. "I don't wish no bad luck on him, though, niggah the seed to my success, know-wha'-I'm-talkin'-'bout?"

"No doubt," Black sighed.

Once they arrived at the rental car agency, Black co-signed for Cool to rent a luxurious Lincoln town car for a week. Afterwards, he followed Black to his crib in Southpark.

CS

While Money lounged around the house, he decided to phone Black. Since his wheels were in the shop, he needed a ride out.

"Wha'd up Black?" Money greeted. "I'm surprised your ass at the crib. Did you pick up Cool yet?"

"Yeah. That niggah right here."

"Let me holla at that niggah," Money said.

"Hol'on," Black paused; calling his homie to the phone.

"Wha'd up though?" Cool responded.

"Come through and scoop your boy...Niggah grounded dawg," Money informed him.

"Done deal dawg," Cool continued, "I got a rental."

"Good, 'cause that niggah Black be trippin' behind his precious Q-45, but he'll probably let you borrow it," Money imagined, as they both chuckled.

Money gave him the directions, and Cool conceded that he would be there shortly before they hung up. There was a knock on Black's door, as it turned out, it was a youngster that lived down the street named Kris. He wanted to play video games.

"Wha'd up Darkvader?" Kris joked, as he entered smiling.

"Ain't shit mellow yellow," Black retorted, as they all laughed.

"Where my bitch Bertha?" Kris signified on Black's mother; a normal ritual among true homeboys.

"Y'all niggahs throwed" Cool intervened, as they all chuckled.

"That's my bitch for real Cool!" Kris shot back, displaying a serious look, as he continued. "They finally let you out that bitch, huh?" he said; giving Cool some dap.

"Yeah...Niggah you don' got big since I been gone!" Cool observed.

"He a big butt boy now," Black intervened comically, "I done turned him out." They all chuckled at his homo remark.

"Emm-hmm, jus' like I turn ya mama out," Kris teased, while they continued to crack on each other.

"Fuck you strawberry," Black fumed.

"Man, I'ma go scoop Money," Cool interrupted; regaining his composure, "y'all boys still throwed. I'ma also shoot through a couple of traps and see what the haps. I be back in a short-short. Need me to pick up somethin' while I'm out?"

"Brang back some Remy," Black said; reaching in his pocket.

"Don't worry B, this one on me," Cool assured, "I'ma holla atcha Kris."

"Ah'ight Cool," Kris replied," if my baby Bertha stop by here I'ma tell her to chill, let cha get a shot of that ass, know-wha'-I'm-talkin'-'bout?"

They all burst out in laughter.

"Fuck you niggah!" Black chuckled. "When he get back, we gon' all run a train on you, 'cause ain't a better joy than a big butt boy," he jived; causing them to crack up in gleeful hysteria, as Cool made his way to the door; shaking his head to their zany antics.

CS

While Cool drove along, he decided to creep through Sunnyside first. When he initially arrived home, he noticed some nice rides sitting in the driveway of a couple of cats he used to serve back in the day. As he cruised down his mom's street, an old affiliate came into view. He rolled down his window to chat briefly, once he approached.

"Wha'd up kinfolk?" Cool greeted.

"Chillin' man," Ken replied; giving him dap, "I heard you was out dawg. I see you still Mr. Flossy. What they hittin for?"

Street rhetoric to Cool's ears, since Ken was a decent cat he could trust. Ken was sort of skittish; dealing and socializing with only a chosen few. Qualities Cool loved. Plus judging by his tricked out rides, as well as gaudy jewelry, business must've been booming.

"Well kinfolk," Cool continued evasively, " I just raised, so I haven't been on the prowl in a while, but when you ready you can hit me at my T-Jones' crib, and I'll see what I can come up wit', kno'-wha'-I'm talkin'-bout?"

"Okay fly guy," Ken chuckled, "but a niggah like me stay ready, that's why I'm screamin' atcha now."

"Whatcha tryna do then?"

"A bird or two, depends on yo' number."

"I see you been handlin' up," Cool praised.

"I ain't been raisin' no hell dawg," Ken replied modestly.

"I can't tell…But I think I can oblige. What you normally pay?"

"Damn niggah! I ask you what they hit for, now you wanna know what I pay! Wanna know where I get it from too?!" Ken wise cracked.

"It ain't like that kinfolk," Cool chuckled, "I'm jus' tryna look out for your best interest, know-wha'-I'm-talkin'-'bout? I wanna give you a better deal so you can fuck wit' me."

"Yuh right. Like I said, still fly as hell," Ken retorted. "I get it for one sixty-five, sometimes one six. Think you can handle that?"

"Gon' have to, if I want your patronage."

CS

As Money waited impatiently, he decided to phone Black to see what was taking Cool so long to arrive.

"Man where that niggah at?!" Money shrieked; immediately after Black answered the phone.

"Hell I don't know, Black vaguely replied, "I thought he was comin' to get you."

"Niggah musta made a detour,"Money questioned.

"Ain't no tellin' 'bout that fool... That niggah did say he was gon' crawl through the 'hood. He probably be pullin' up in a few. When he get there, tell him don't forget the Remy," Black ordered

"Ah'ight fuckin' drunk," Money responded.

They both hung up.

CS

Meanwhile, Ken and Cool was still busy collaborating, Cool decided to string his bait along in anticipation of Ken's business.

"Gimme 'bout an hour baby boy, I promise, I'ma look out for you, jus' gimme yo' digits" Cool affirmed.

"Bet that, let me go get a pen. Niggah you still ain't tol' me what you chargin'?" Ken reiterated.

"Don't sweat it, I gotcha dawg. I want it to be a surprise, jus' don't go around the corner on my ass, kno'-wha'-I'm-talkin'-'bout?"

"I ain't trippin', even though I hate fuckin' surprises. Jus' make sure it's some good ye-yo," Ken said, as he headed inside the house to get a pen.

"I'll assure it's A-1 yola 'cause that's the way we rolla!" Cool screamed with rhythm.

"Whaatevah!" Ken blurted back in the distance with a chuckle.

After Cool retrieved the number, he sped off confirming his word was bond. He beamed within, because he had not been out forty-eight hours yet and was already progressing. He bobbed his head to the music of the rappers called: Eightball and MJG, as he cruised toward Money's house.

CS

Since Money only lived fifteen minutes on the out-skirts of the 'hood, Cool made it there in no time. Money was waiting outside all G'd up, with an in explicable look on his face. Cool knew exactly what was about to be said, as he hopped in the car displaying his embellished gold and diamond grill.

"Damn kinfolk!" Money began, "I thought" you was cut off.

"Naw, niggah, I ain't get lost, my sense of direction ain't like our boy Ray," Cool smirked, as they both chuckled.

"No shit," Money replied "that boy been livin' in Houston umpteen years and still gets lost." They both agreed mutually. "Black said don't forget the Remy."

"That alcoholic fucka called you 'bout that?" Cool smirked

"Naw. I called him wonderin' where your ass was, and his booze head ass reminded me," Money wisecracked.

"He jus' like his boy Ray ain't he?" Cool chuckled.

"Yeah, that niggah ain't gon' never change," Money sighed,

"I feel ya". Cool transitioned. "Ya know that niggah Kris somthin' else."

"Yeah, you musta seen that fool at Black's crib?"

"Mm-hm"

"That's all them knuckle heads wanna do is play video games all day. Was that niggah Frank over there too?"

"Who, Kris uncle fat ass?' Cool remarked.

"Yuh," Money chuckled.

"No, but I know he gon' be tryna rank on a niggah when I see him, fat fucka!"

They both chuckled, as they pulled in to a liquor store, about five minutes from Black's house. Cool strolled inside, leaving Money behind, and purchased a half gallon of Remy Martin VSOP, cups, and a bag of ice. On his way back to the car, Money gawked; dazzled by the huge bottle in Cool's hand.

"Oh shit niggah! Whatcha tryna do, get the 'hood high?"

"Naw, not yet anyway," Cool chuckled, as Money smiled. "We still celebratin' my niggah, besides it keeps us from runnin' back and forth to the sto', know-wha'-I'm-talkin'-'bout?"

"You got a point my niggah," Money conceded.

"Anyway. Where yo' wheels, you still got the MPV, huh?" Cool asked curiously.

"Ain't no secret," Money boasted proudly, "I'm getting' a couple of woofers, an' some t.v. screens put in it by you know who."

"You must be talkin' 'bout o' punk ass Terry," Cool smirked knowingly, "he the shit, but he think a niggah 'pose to kiss his ass."

"A niggah will kick him in the ass," Money sneered, as they both chuckled.

Pulling in Black's driveway, Cool pondered the price Black would charge for the two kilos he was about to ask him for. Hopefully, they could agree on a tight price; pleasing Ken, while concurrently reaping a substantial enough profit for himself. Money was busy on the cellular phoning Black to let them in. Black came to the door grumbling, as they were getting out the car.

"Damn niggahs, took y'all long enough! Where my shit at?!" Black complained jokingly.

"Chill baby boy I got yo' fix," Cool chuckled, as he continued, "a niggah been tryna make a few power moves, know-wha'-I'm-talkin'-'bout?"

They all stepped inside the house, made themselves drinks, and resumed playing video games. After a few minutes of chill time, Cool observed the clock on Black's desk; noticing it was time to fulfill his appointment with Ken.

"Look out Black," Cool began,grasping his attention, "I ran into one of my kinfolks from back in the game, an' the niggah mentioned coppin' a couple bricks."

Black abruptly paused the video game, and strolled toward the kitchen; stating he needed more ice in his drink. Cool analyzed the oddity of his homie's demeanor; letting his conscience be his guide, and followed behind Black accordingly. He had a gut feeling his homie was trying to disguise something.

"Say man, I'ma play the game wit' Kris, you holdin' up anotha niggah turn!" Money shouted in the distance.

"Go 'head dawg!" Black continued. "He saved yo' ass Kris!"

"Niggah please!..I was gon' come back! You only ten ahead" Kris shot back with an assertive stance.

As they resumed battling on Madden, Black and Cool were busy conferring on their next course of events – in contriving fashion.

"I didn't wanna discuss no prices in there wit' them niggahs." Black uttered.

"I kinda figured that," Cool chuckled knowingly, that's why I followed yo' ass."

"Who the niggah that wanna score?" Black replied skeptically.

"Don't gimme that look dawg," Cool leered knowingly, "he straight, ya know I know how to get down kinfolk."

"Aw niggah, I know that," Black smirked, "I just wanted to know who the niggah is" as he downplayed his paranoia.

"No doubt," Cool continued, "you remember the cat who live down the street from my T-Jones?"

"Yeah, I remember homeboy," Black sighed as he diverted topics, "since we gon' be business partners soon, I want cha to kno' I be getting the shit for fou'teen. So whatever profit you make off Ken, we could jus' split it down the middle. Try to make a thousand profit off each brick, though…an' always feel free to make mo'."

"Ain't no question playa," Cool stressed, "That shit goes without saying."

"Then, when we get som' mo', we gon' bus' a couple down," Black continued. "Slangin' them zones is how we gon' make most our ends anyway."

"I feel you kinfolk," Cool agreed, "I got a couple of reliable prospects outta town too. I plan to Uncle Sam em'."

"Suppose to."

"Ken tol' me he normally pay sixteen, so I'll charge him fi'teen five, puttin' my baitin' process in effect, kno'-wha'-I'm-talkin'-bout?"

"Shh…that's still tight fool," Black lauded his homie's tactics, as he continued, "that mean we make three thousand; fi'teen hun' a piece babyboy. I'm wit' it, so when the nig' wanna get it?"

"Right now," Cool assured.

"It's all good dawg," Black continued, "since we choppin' it up dawg, I wantcha to know that the supply stay at it's peak."

"Dig that," Cool agreed, "but what that time frame like?"

"Ain't no pa'ticular time," Black assured, "time is on our side…I mean, as it flo', we jus' simply pay our debt."
Cool chuckled at his statement, giving Black some dap.

"Ah'ight ," Cool transitioned, "well, ain't no need in me dawdlin' around here. The only game I wanna play is wit' them ol' dead green guys." They both cackled at his eagerness. "So, how far is it to the shit?" he asked comically.

"Look there in the trash can," Black gestured chucklingly.

"In the trash can?" Cool grimaced. He scoured the trash vigorously – to no avail. Until Black informed him the product was ensconced under the trash bag itself. To his surprise there were three well taped kilos at the bottom. "Damn man! We need a crib for real," he emphasized.

"It's all good" Black continued. "I ain't have but a few left, I knew they was gon' fly, so I didn't even bother takin' em' to Money's crib like I normally do."

"Fuck 'round and take the trash out, an' forget about them mu'fuckas," Cool quipped.

"Fuck you niggah, I ain't Ray!" Black hissed, as they both chuckled. "I dunno when them damn fools comin' wit' the rest, but you can have two of them. We really need that car too, so a niggah can start puttin' it down the way we 'pose to." Cool nodded in agreement.

"Dig that," Cool conceded, " I'ma get Money to roll wit' me jus' in case som' shit jump off…Hm, break out like Carl Lewis if I have to, feel me?" They both chuckled, knowing he was serious about hurtling off, if problems occurred. "Let me call my niggah an make sure he wanna deuce 'em up, fi'teen five should move him."

"Handle up dawg," Black urged, "remember not to pimp our hand to the homies."

"I ain't trippin'," Cool smirked. "I know how the damn thang go. But whatcha be chargin' them niggahs. I mean, a niggah don't wanna put his foot in his mouth… jus' in case they do confront me."

"Enough said," Black continued, "I be lettin' 'em get it for sixteen."

"Aw niggah, that ain't bad," Cool continued, "Wha'd up with Kris, he in the game too?"

"That yellow hammer have licks every now an' then," Black quipped, as they both chuckled. "I be givin' that niggah a few zones here an' there, nothin' major. Petty flo', but it all add up, ya know."

"Well, let me hit this damn fool, an' see if he ready," Cool sighed, "it's like they say kinfolk, some is better than none."

As Cool got the number from his pocket to phone Ken, Black strolled to the backroom to resume playing the video game.

"Hello, may I speak with Ken?" Cool cordially asked; unable to decipher the voice.

"This me man, wha'd up?" Ken eagerly replied.

"I didn't recognize yo' voice dawg," Cool chuckled, "I think I can oblige" he continued with an aura of confidence. "How does one fi'ty five sound?"

"That's straight!" Ken beamed. "I'ma duce 'em up too."

"Well kinfolk, I can be there in fi'teen. You wit' it?" Cool replied confidently.

"Make it twenty-five, so I can get my shit together."

After Cool hung up, he strolled to the back elated by the consummation of his first deal. Since the road ahead had begun to look lucrative, he decided to trouble Black about other imperative necessities.

"Look out Black," Cool blurted, "I'ma need a pager an' cell phone. Hook a niggah up!"

"Niggah who you think I am, yo' fuckin' fairy Godfather?!" Black retorted. "You gon' have to spread your hustle niggah."

"I ain't trippin'. I'm jus' not tryna put them shits in my name, know-wha'-I'm-talkin'-'bout? Cool warned. "I guess I can get a broad to cop them joints."

"Black get that man a phone…I betcha if it was one of them hoes, yo' black ass would do it" Kris implied, as Black quickly cut him short.

"Niggah you don't know what I can get o' vanilla ass niggah!" Black hissed.

Everybody chuckled.

"Let me find out," Kris began comically; leering directly at Black, as he continue, "you been hangin' 'round the room eaves droppin' when I be fuckin' yo' mama. That's the same thang she be callin' me when I'm jumpin' up down in that pussy."

They all cracked up. The vulgar antics caused Money to spill some of his drink unintentionally.

"Fuck you!" Black shot the middle finger, as he continued chuckling, "yo' mama don't call me nothin' at all, bitch can't talk wit' a dick in her mouth!"

They all continued to roar with laughter, pausing the video game while Kris and Black commenced to rank on each other's mothers; until a knock at the door subdued the energy.

"Y'all here that?" Money questioned dubiously.

"It's somebody at the door," Black assured, as he strolled off to see who it was. "Who is it?" he asked peering out the peephole knowingly.

"It's me niggah!" Ray announced. "Let me in!"

"I don't know no fuckin' me!" Black joked. "You better say yo' name dawg before I blast!"

Ray cackled at his antics.

"Open up the door Blacky!" Ray bellowed boisterously.

On that note, he opened the door for his homie.

"You finish for today dawg?" Black asked seriously.

"Yuh, that's it." Ray slurred, "it's Miller time."

"Soun' like you already had Miller time," Black smirked. "That niggah Cool in there."

"Where my niggah at?!" Ray beamed, as they strolled to the back.

"Ray-Ray, what's goin down baby?!" Cool shouted in the distance.

Once Ray stepped in the doorway, Cool was standing there to greet him with a brotherly hug.

"What's up man?!" Ray said excitedly.

"Tryna live baby boy!" Cool continued, as the homies observed. "Why you ain't show up at the comin home party?!"

"I betcha Brenda wouldn't let his ass out, huh?" Kris added.

They all teased Ray, aware of his henpecked way of living. His girlfriend allowed him rights sporadically; making him the odd ball of the faction.

"Fuck all y'all!" Ray slurred with a grin.

"Damn kinfolk," Cool bantered, "you been drinkin' on the job?"

"I ain't had nothin' yet," Ray assured as everybody scrutinized him laughingly.

"Well, I got a treat for you," Cool said; holding up the half gallon bottle, "go get you a cup damn fool!"

"Already!" Ray beamed; strolling off to fetch a cup; while the homie snickered; knowing liquor to him was like toys to kids on Christmas Day.

"Look out Money," Cool announced, "drive me to go hit this lick."

"It's all gravy" Money replied willingly.

"Let's dip dawg," Cool continued. "Ray, that bottle bet not be empty by the time I get back, you fuckin' lush."

They all chuckled.

"Fuck you niggah," Ray gibbered with a smile, "you bet not be long then!"

They all laughingly shook their heads in ridicule at Ray's comment, as Cool and Money headed off; leaving their drinks behind as a precaution; before they went to serve the illicit goods.

CS

As they cruised along almost to their destination, Cool decided to phone Ken to make sure matters were in order.

"You got your celly on you, huh?" Cool asked as he continued. "Make sure e'erythang-e'erythang before we get too far, "know-wha'-I'm-talkin'-'bout?'

"Already," Money replied; pulling the phone out of his pocket. "Niggah ain't tryna make no blank trips, bad enough we takin' penitentiary chances."

"No doubt," Cool agreed. "Hello, may I speak with Ken?" he asked once the phone stopped ringing.

"He went to the store," the mysterious voice replied.

"Damn!" Cool blurted, as Money observed.

"Who's this?" the voice asked.

"This Cool," he responded.

"Oh what's up Cool? This his uncle J.P., he told me to tell you to come on by, he'll be back in a minute."

"I thought he forgot about me. Tell him when he get back to stay put... By the way, how you been ol' timer?"

"Same ol' shit," J.P. replied as he continued, " I'll be sure to tell him you're on the way."

"Ah'ight. Good lookin' out."

"No problem. Bye." J.P. said, as they both hung up.

Money frowned; bewildered by what was discussed, he intrusively began to ask questions.

"Wha happen dawg!?" Money interjected menacingly. "Don't tell me that cake ass niggah wasn't there."

"Naw e'erythang straight kinfolk," Cool assured, "he made a move right quick."

"That fucka bounced?! Aw, hell naw, I'ma!.." Money began to get irate.

"Calm down clown, he on his way back, cut the brethren some slack," Cool chuckled defensively.

As they pulled in Ken's driveway, Money noticed a car within his view.

"Look out dawg, is that that niggah right there?" Money uttered; averting his attention toward the oncoming vehicle.

"Yuh that's my peeps, chill baby boy, I'll be back!" Cool joked; mimicking Arnold from the Terminator movie.

"You retarded dawg," Money chuckled; shaking his head.

Cool hopped out the car with his shirt tail hanging out, camouflaging the product hidden in his pants.

"Wha'd up though?' Cool spoke; giving Ken dap, as he approached him. "I thought you sent me on a blank trip for a minute there kinfolk."

"Never that," Ken smirked, "ya know I don't get down like that. I jus' had to cop me a few supplies, I hope it's all good when I test the shit"

"No doubt. It's jus' business kinfolk, besides, it would be ludicrous for you not to," Cool affirmed.

"Ah'ight my niggah let's do this," Ken stressed; leading the way inside.

Once inside Cool cased the unclean surroundings.

"Look out kinfolk," Cool continued, as they entered the kitchen, "jus' take fou'teen grams outta each. If that shit boo-boo, I'll take it back an' get you two mo'. I'm sure it's straight, though."

"We'll see ina minute dawg," Ken replied, as he prepped for the test. "I see you big daddy," he joked, "just raised and puttin' it down like it go. Let me find out you had some shit stashed while you was gone."

"I wouldn't say all that kinfolk," Cool grinned, "but when you're indispensable, a niggah wit' solid principles, you reap the playa made benefits you deserve, know-wha'-I'm-talkin'-'bout?"

"I feel you playboy," Ken lauded his axiom; simultaneously grinning, as he continued, "you still the flyest thang since the airplane, huh?"

"It don't stop till the casket drop," Cool boasted; giving him dap, "I thought you knew."

As Cool cut the top of both kilos with a knife, Ken pulled out a digital scale from the cabinet. Then, he stepped aside and let Ken carve fourteen grams out of each brick. With a content look on his mug, Ken scrutinized the layers of shiny crystals that were displayed within both bricks. Ken put fourteen grams in each pyrex glass measuring jar that sat on the counter, then added two teaspoons of Arm and Hammer baking soda to each. After that, he added a little water in both, then put them in the microwave on five minutes. While the dope was still hot, Ken took a fork and stirred both substances vigorously for a couple of seconds. Then, he splashed tap water meticulously over each jar until both had a jelly like substance that subsided to the bottom. His last step was placing them on the counter in a slightly tilted angle. This method was prudent in his attempt to make the dope transform into two half cookies – once it hardened up.

"Hol'up!" Ken beamed. "It's that pineapple color shit too!" he expressed: Knowing his clientele flocked to this particular kind.

"Don't say I didn't warn you niggah," Cool quipped; judging his homie's excited look. "Now where my chips?" he demanded.

"Hol' that down dawg, ya know I gotcha," Ken promised.

Ken placed each kilo-one at a time – on the scale to make sure the weight was at least a thousand grams a piece. By the time he finished that, the crack was ready. He poured the excess water out of each jar with the look of a mad scientist, as he examined his work.

"Now ya happy niggah?" Cool uttered impatiently.

"Eureka baby boy!" Ken expressed, as they both chuckled.

"Now you can get my evil faces together," Cool suggested, "I gotta dip, in pursuit of otha interests."

"Ah'ight chief," Ken smirked, "I ain't gon' hol' ya up. Jus' make sure it stay this way."

Afterwards, Ken retrieved a brown paper bag from the pantry, handing it to Cool. Cool copped a squat at the dinette table counting the rubber band stacks of twenties, fifties, and hundreds with the poise of a bank teller.

CS

Meanwhile, Money sat in the ride with the engine running, bobbing his head to a tape he had pulled from his pocket. It was a mixtape by D.J. Screw – the tempo so slow that some people had to be high to relate. As he was relishing H-Town 'hood music, his phone rang disturbing his groove.

"Yeah," Money answered nonchalant.

"Wha'd up, you niggahs ah'ight?' Black queried; checking up on his minions.

"We straight," Money assured, "I see Cool comin' out the door now, we be back ina minute."

"Jus makin' sure y'all straight."

"Ah'ight big head Black," Money signified, as they hung up.

Cool strolled back to the car throwing up the deuce to Ken, and waved bye to his uncle before they drove off.

Chapter – 6

I t was dusk dark by the time Cool and Money made it back to Black's house. Ray and Kris had vamoosed, but at least Ray didn't drink all the Remy. Black's wife along with his two adorable little girls, was there as well. Before they got out the car to go inside, Money phoned Black; making him aware of their presence.

"Shawana!" Black screamed from the back room. "Open the door for Cool and Money!"

"They out there now?!" Shawana bellowed back.

"Yup!" he assured.

She strolled toward the door halting her house chores.

"Hey" Shawana greeted cordially, as she opened the door, "I see they finally let you go, huh Carlos?"

"Yup. You doin' ah'ight?" Cool replied.

"I'm fine, just tryna get some of our things packed up for the movers," Shawana diverted. "How are you doin' Money?"

"I'm tight, jus' tryna stay sucka free," Money bantered.

"Where them girls at?" Cool added. "I know they done got bigger."

"And badder too," Shawana expressed, as they all chuckled, "you'll probably bump into 'em on the way to the back."

"Ah'ight. Why Black ain't helpin'?" Cool jived knowingly.

"That lazy niggah!" Shawana snapped, as they chuckled. "He'll just be in the way anyway."

As they strolled toward the back, Cool pondered Shawana's cliché about her husband. He knew Black wouldn't help. Dope dealers don't do labor, they'd rather pay someone instead. An innate deficiency commonplace to street hustlers. As they approached Black's office/ room, Black's two little girls came into view.

"Wha'd up kinfolk, you look pregnant?" Black joked.

"Lucky these kids in here, "Cool mumbled briefly, as he diverted his attention toward the little girls. "Hello there beautiful ladies, y'all remember me?"

The girls stood still; dubiously trying to figure out who Cool was; with huge smiles displayed on their faces.

"They done got big, huh?" Money said.

"An' bad too," Black reiterated his wife's phrase, "they in here drivin' me crazy, askin' all kind of shit...Y'all gon' in there wit' yo' mama, daddy will talk to y'all later...Okay? Tell Money and Cool bye."

Shontay and Shere´, submissively waved on their way out.

"What you got good in that belly of yours," Black said with a grin.

Black knew Cool's sudden pregnancy stored the loot he had just accumulated. On that note, Cool pulled the paper bag from underneath his shirt.

"I took mine off top, kinfolk. I flipped through it too, it should be straight," Cool informed.

"I feel you, I'll get to it later," Black responded; tossing the bag in his closet on top of a safe that was bolted to the floor.

A knock at the door stole their attention.

"Let me go see who at the door," Black announced, "that might be our goodies." Black shouted once he made it to the door."Lookout they here!" Black announced with a black duffel bag in his hand. "Y'all come check the wheels out!"

The bag contained the product Black been expecting. Jim slipped it through the burglar bars, as soon as he opened the door.

"Let's go peep the ride kinfolk," Cool said to Money, as he stood up with a mirthful expression on his face.

"'Bout time them niggahs showed up," Money replied, as he tailed behind.

While they scampered toward the front, they were both elated, because the car would play an important role in their dastardly deeds.

"Damn Jim baby, it took y'all long enough!" Cool indicated once he made it outside; simultaneously giving him some dap.

"I been runnin' aroun' all day brotha," Jim sighed, "I apologize for the delay," he continued sincerely. "I probably coulda made it sooner, but I had to wait on Hank slow ass to get the car."

"It ain't shit," Cool down-played. "So this o' Hank, huh? Wha'd up though?" he greeted; giving the new comer some dap; while Black and Money were busy inspecting the family's new transportation.

"You the one jus' got out, huh?" Hank asked vaguely.

"Yeah, that's me, back from hell dawg," Cool quipped.

"Dig that," Hank emphasized, "I know how it is, trus', I just got out last year. What facility they had you at?"

"Some bu'shit," Cool stressed, "it was a camp though, laid back for the most part, no gate around it, but the mu'fucka also got too many tedious rules," he emphasized.

"I feel you," Hank chuckled, "I heard about those camps. You musta didn't have much time, huh?"

" Nope, thank God for that," Cool replied gratefully.

"Man this mu'fucka got a lot of miles on it!" Black announced; getting everyone's attention.

"You ain't never satisfied o' purple ass niggah!" Hank retorted fiercely, "ya know the car wasn't gon' be brand new!"

Everybody mutually chuckled at his statement.

"Aw you o' football head bastard, I know it wasn't gon' be new, it's a fuckin' hand me down!" Black stressed.

"Goddamn!" Money snapped, getting their attention as he browsed the trunk. "Black, Cool, get over here dawg!" They all stepped to the trunk, curious. "Look!"

"What's wrong wit' you niggah!" Black grimaced; leading the pack

"This shit infested wit' roaches!" Money roared, as he fell out laughing.

"Where at dawg?!" Cool responded, as they were almost in view of the rodents.

"Man, y'all some triflin' bastards!" Black grimaced laughingly. "I bet it got all kind of chicken bones, layin' 'round in this bitch!" he fussed, as they all chuckled. "I know Jerry fat greedy ass got somethin' to do wit' this! We gon' have to exterminate this mu'fucka, tell that fat fuc' I want a discount!" he humored in serious fashion.

"We jus' deliver dawg," Hank retorted defensively, "you gon' have to take that up wit' big boy, besides, niggah, you own a pest control business."

"Hank," Black uttered contemptuously, "ya know damn well exterminating vehicles ain't commonplace, so don't even try that bullshit!"

They all laughed, as Cool and Money scoured the interior.

"Man it's roaches all over this bitch!" Money grimaced.

"That's a damn shame kinfolk," Cool observed; shaking his head in ridicule.

"We just gon' have to bomb this mu'fucka," Black intervened, "here Jim, give this to him!" he said as he pulled a baby wade of currency from his pocket, tossing it from a short distance.

"How much is this?" Jim asked curiously; scanning the measly rubber band stack.

"Twenty five hun'ed," Black replied, "tell him I'll have the rest later, hell, he ain't gon' do nothin' but fuck it off anyway."

"Already," Hank agreed.

"Oh, I almost' forgot... I got some mo' scratch for y'all, Black responded, as he transitioned. "Let me holla atcha Cool!"

Black and Cool strolled back inside the house leaving the rest behind.

"What's goin' down?" Cool uttered curiously, once they were inside.

"You said you counted the change you gave me, huh?" Black affirmed.

"No doubt baby boy," Cool assured, "should be twenty-nine five, like I tol' you I took my fi'teen off top, ya dig."

"Ah'ight, I'ma give it to these fools so they can get on outta here, they can count it their damn self," Black scoffed, as he headed toward the back room to retrieve the cash.

Cool stepped back outside as Black headed to the back. Once he made it to where the cash was, he took five hundred out of it, making it an even twenty-nine thousand. He then took his portable organizer and properly adjusted his tally deducting twenty-nine thousand and adding the cost of five kilos to the existing balance. He strolled back outside with the loot stashed under his shirt, disguised from the intrusive public view of his neighbors.

"Tell that doughnut belly mu'fucka that's twenty-nine thousand," Black jeered, as he sat in Jim's car to hand over the cash.

They cackled at his roasting remark.

"Ah'ight man," Jim chuckled, "here the extra set of keys to the hoop', we gon' bounce dawg, ya know we still ridin' dirty."

"I feel you," Black continued, "gon' handle your business and be careful."

They all gave each other dap, before Jim and Hank departed. Then they locked up the dope mobile and strolled in the house.

"Put this shit up for me dawg, it should be five of 'em there," Black ordered, as he picked up the bag of kilos he left in the hallway earlier. "I'ma need y'all to run an errand."

CS

Cruising along test-driving the family's new vehicle, Cool and Money small talked about the facts of life. Their destination was only a short distance away, but they still hoped the other party was there waiting, so they could garner the cash and vamoose in a timely fashion.

"Look out kinfolk," Money continued, "after we finish hittin' this stang, drop me off at the ponderosa."

"Wha'd up dawg, you don't wanna hang out wit'cha homie?" Cool asked jokingly.

"No my niggah, that ain't it," Money sighed, "it's family night tonight, an' I try to spend a little quality time wit' 'em, so shit stay right."

"Aw that's so sweet," Cool teased, as Money displayed his middle finger.

"Don't even go there, you know a niggah be deep in the streets dawg," Money ranted.

"Dig that. I ain't trippin', you s'pose to spen' time with your love ones, my niggah that's real shit."

Tomorrow we gon' go to Foxes though, it's a joint where them boppas be workin' at," Money assured, "don't be trippin' like you did atcha comin' home party niggah," he quipped; as he inserted the same mix tape they were listening to in the rental car earlier.

"I wasn't trippin' then kinfolk, jus' had my mind on my money, an' my money on my mind, know-wha'-I'm-talkin'-'bout?" Cool replied, as he continued. "Aw not that shit again," he expressed; as the slow tempo tunes blasted from the stereo.

"That's that Screw goin' down," Money stressed.

"Yeah, it's all good, I know the shit will rub off on me eventually," Cool chuckled.

"No doubt," Money replied, bobbing his head slowly, as Cool leered at him.

"Man you crazy," Cool grinned. "My niggah, we don't even know what kinfolk ridin' in, hit Black an' see what the deal."

"At leas' I know how the niggah look," Money responded, as he dialed Black's number, "but I donno what kind of slab he got though."

As they arrived at the Timmy Chan restaurant, they deemed it best to place their orders at the take out window; instead of dealing with the congested inside lobby.

"I see that barn yard pimp still black folks favorite dish," Cool observed, as they both chuckled at his statement.

"Ain't a damn thang change kinfolk, this mu'fucka still be pack'd wit' hungry niggahs, hell, I still visit occasionally my damn self," Money quipped, as he held the phone waiting on Black to answer.

Cool chuckled as he finally approached the over crowded take out window. "Look out Money," Cool sighed. "You want some of this shit?"

"Welcome to Timmy Chan may I help you?" a female ghetto sounding voice intervened over the intercom.

"Gimme a minute," Cool shot back. "Wha'd up though, my niggah?" he asked in Money's direction.

"I'll pass my nig'," Money rejected, "if I get full an' my wife cooked, that's my ass." They both chuckled, as he still waited for Black to answer his phone. "I'll jus' nibble on a lil of yo shit."

"Dig that. I ain't tryna eat all this greasy shit."

Finally getting in contact with Black, Money asked a few questions while Cool ordered the food. Afterwards, he pulled around to the next window to pick it up.

"We probably a li'l early dawg," Money said, as he hung up with Black. "He just said his kinfolk know what we in, but he forgot to ask dude what kind of slab he was gon' be in, ya dig?"

Cool shook his head in ridicule. "That was very bright of him, huh?" They both chuckled.

"He also said to look for a black Maxima or a black Ford F-150 pick up, the niggah might be rollin' in either one of them," Money assured.

After Cool retrieved the grub, he pulled in a parking space on the blind side of the building. The low key drug mobile they were riding in blended perfectly with the other myriad of patrons in the parking lot. Earlier, when Black and Cool stepped inside the house to have their little tête-à-tête, Jim showed Money how to use the hidden compartment. Money had stashed the three kilos inside; initially before they departed. At Black's house, Cool didn't quite comprehend how the apparatus worked, but he would soon find out once De Wayne arrived, he thought, while he devoured the chicken wings and rice greedily.

"This shit on hit baby boy," Cool laughed; licking his fingers.

"Dig that," Money agreed, "whatever they put in this shit keep a niggah comin' back for mo'." They both chuckled knowingly.

"When o' boy get here, I want you to show me how to pop the spot." Cool said, trying to talk with a mouth full of food.

"No doubt," Money continued, "that niggah Jim showed me how to work it when y'all duck'd in the house earlier," he assured; with a mouth full of food also.

As they continued eating, they scrutinized a black car that fit the description pulling into the parking lot suddenly. When the vehicle pulled next to theirs; rolling down the window, Cool did the same.

"What's up baby boy?" DeWayne greeted.

"It's all good," Cool replied, as he continued, "you must be the cat we been waitin' on?"

"I'm Black homeboy DeWayne, let's do this, I don't have to tell you how hot it is 'round here," De Wayne stressed.

"My sentiments exactly," Cool concurred, "gimme a minute," he said, as he rolled back up the window.

On that note Money took a staple from the ashtray and commence to demonstrating the mechanics of the stash spot.

"Peep game baby boy," Money whispered, "you take this staple and stick one end of it in the top part, and the otha end in the bottom part of the diagnostic socket underneath the dash, like this. Make sure you touch both ends at the same time, metal to metal." He then inserted the metal instrument into the makeshift socket, until sparks flew and a pop noise came from the right side quarter panel, Cool observed with an amazed look on his mug. "There it is my niggah," he said with an eureka expression, "the left sockets in the switch is for the left stash, an' the right side is for the right stash."

"Hol' up man," Cool chuckled; flattered by the street technology. "Now, that's what I call niggah riggin' at its finest." They both chuckled giving each other dap, as Money retrieved the kilos from the immense size hole. "I can get use to this James Bond shit."

"Already," Money replied, as he reentered the front seat, handing Cool the bag of kilos.

Cool grabbed the illicit package, tucked it under his shirt, and hopped out to do the deal in De Wayne's ride; hoping big brother was having a doughnut break; instead of surveilling his felonious deed. Good thing the windows were tinted dark, he thought.

"Wha'd up kinfolk? They call me Cool," Cool greeted; giving De Wayne dap, as he flopped in the passenger seat.

"So, you the one been on lock, huh?" De Wayne replied knowingly; handing him a black leather bag.

"That's right," Cool shot back; sliding him the narcotics. "You don't waste no time, huh?" De Wayne smirked.

"I've wasted enough of that, ya dig?" Cool retorted.

"I feel ya," De Wayne chuckled, "well let me be out. Tell that damn fool if he have any problems to hit me on the hip."

"Like wise," Cool responded; giving him dap, as he casually strolled back to his car with the leather bag.

Before De Wayne tipped off, he bellowed out the window about the return of his bag on their next rendezvous.

"E'erythang-e'erythang?" Money asked, as Cool reentered the car.

"E'erythang kool-aid kinfolk, put the chedda' up," Cool replied, hurling the bag from a short distance.

The stash spot was so roomy it engulfed the entire bag with ease. They decided to rid themselves of the loot before Cool dropped Money off at home, as they now approaching Black's house.

"Hold it down dawg, let me run in here and give Black this change," Cool said, as they pulled in the driveway. He then took the staple out of the ashtray to open the compartment. "Is this how you do it kinfolk," he questioned; fumbling inside the socket.

"Yeah, jus' make sure you touch metal to metal until sparks fly," Money replied, as he fired up a blunt stashed away in his shirt pocket.

"I heard it pop man!" Cool enthused; with an accomplished look on his mug.

Cool knew it was a possibility he could get broke off a portion of the profit Black received from De Wayne, since he had decided to make him a partner.

"It's open baby boy, you done it," Money uttered with a mouth full of smoke.

"Sometime soon we need to put an alarm on this bitch, jus' to be safe than sorry, know-wha'-I'm-talkin'-'bout?" Cool suggested.

"Sounds logical to me," Money agreed, as he continued getting high.

"Hit that niggah, and tell him to let me in dawg," Cool said, as he grabbed the food and the loot before he got out the car.

By the time Cool approached the front door, Black emerged instantaneously.

"I take it e'erythang went well?" Black asked, as he let Cool in.

"If the niggah scrilla ain't counterfeit we straight. Otha than that, I'm here ain't I?" Cool retorted.

"Ah'ight ol' sarcastic ass niggah," Black chuckled, seriously. "Look dawg, I might as well help you shine out the gate. Besides, I jus' got half of your stang."

"So what you sayin', is that from here on out, I got fi'ty/fi'ty action?" Cool asked.

"That's exactly what I'm sayin' damn fool," Black shot back.

"'Preciate you baby boy," Cool beamed; giving him dap. "Ya know I ain't gon' letcha down, might brang you up, but never letcha down."

They both chuckled at his sincere statement.

Black dumped the cash that Cool had brought back from the deal on his bed and commenced to counting it. The cash was stacked in thousand dollar bundles; facilitating the calculating process.

"Here you go my niggah," Black paused, handing Cool three rubber band stacks, "I charged that fool sixteen, so that mean three thousand a piece."

"Good lookin'," Cool responded with a grin, as he pondered how productive the day had been for him. "Let me go drop this damn fool off dawg, I'll be back ina minute, niggah talkin'-'bout it's family night or some shit."

"That's what that pussy said?" Black bantered, as they both snickered walking toward the front door.

"Yeah," Cool chuckled, "an' I don't want his wife to be holdin' no grudges against me."

"Gotta blame it on somebody, hell," Black joked, as they both chuckled at his sarcastic way of thinking. "How the car ride?"

"Shit, I can sum that up wit' three words... Love it man!" Cool stressed, as they both chuckled.

CS

As Cool cruised along the freeway, he decided to crack the windows a tad bit. Clearing out the rancid smell of reefer that permeated throughout the interior.

"I'm glad you decided to fire up after we finish workin'," Cool complained.

"Jus' 'cause I smoke, don't mean I'm stupid niggah. After the job done, then ya have fun." Money hypothesized.

"Dig that," Cool chuckled, "I was jus' checkin'."

"I got my mind right kinfolk," Money assured.

"Ya know that Screw shit rubbin' off on me," Cool conceded; bobbing his head now to a Tupac song with a slow tempo. "Now I see where y'all get that thug passion shit from."

"Yeah my nig', Tupac invented it," Money smiled; cracking up off the effect the music was having on his homie.

"I wonder what Angel been up to?" Cool mused suddenly.

"Who's that?" Money asked curiously.

"My cuz Red ol' broad." Cool shot in Money's direction. "Damn niggah, you done smok'd that whole blunt!"

"Damn right!" Money yelped, as he revealed his Chinese eyes under his Gucci frame shades. "I look fuc'd up don't I?" he chuckled gleefully.

"At best," Cool informed, "I don't guess none of that shit seep through a niggah system. Ya think?"

"Hell naw o'scary ass niggah," Money grimaced, "we gotta be twenty deep ina phone booth for that kinda shit to happen."

"Call it whatcha want to niggah, but I ain't tryna have no dirty piss," Cool cautioned.

"I feel you," Money agreed, "Yo cuz Red the one that got killed, right?" he changed topics.

"That's who I was talkin'-'bout," Cool replied.

"That's fuc'd up. I heard it was one of them punk ass niggahs he used to run wit'," Money sympathized.

"I heard the same thang, but ya know that niggah was a wild thang, bustin' caps was his hobby. I hate he had to go out like that, though, a niggah of his caliber coulda been worthy of my endeavors," Cool contemplated. "I'ma contact Angel later on, and get the 411 from her, maybe she can clear up some of the madness surrounding this shit," he said.

"Dig that. It's always good to have a few lunatics on the payroll." Money grimaced.

"No doubt," Cool chuckled knowingly. "I think that's what I'll do tonight." he sighed.

"What's that, damn fool?" Money asked intrusively.

"I'ma shoot to the northside and holla at Angel. I ain't doin' shit else for today."

They were now pulling in Money's driveway.

"You can keep my celly... I ain't gon' need it no mo' tonight," Money obliged generously, as he got out the car.

"Good lookin' out my niggah," Cool thanked him.

CS

While Black watched CNN News, sipping on some Remy Martin, his phone rang. It was Cool informing him that he was in the vicinity. After Cool hung up, he pondered his first day of work, and was content with the forty-five hundred dollars he had garnered over a four-hour span. The game was more lucrative than ever before, he thought, as he continued pondering about how long it takes the average working class individual to earn a dope man's salary. He smirked in ridicule knowing the average laborer couldn't compete. Unless, they were top paid executives and even they had to feel Uncle Sam's gluttonous wrath.

As Cool approached the door he noticed it ajar. He strolled in indiscreetly; making his way toward the back where Black was laughing.

"Niggah you better quit leavin' your door open like that," Cool warned, as he poured himself some of the Remy Martin sitting on Black's desk.

"I ain't never slippin' niggah," Black sneered; pulling a snub nose, 357 Magnum from under his mattress.

"Dig that," Cool smirked, "but you need to keep that mu'fucka within range kinfolk, under the bed is too far, know-wha'-I'm-talkin'-'bout?"

"Whaatevah, niggah, you call, so I left the door open for you, I ain't trippin' damn fool," Black transitioned suddenly. "So what happen between you and Trina man?" he asked; taking a swig of his drink.

"Your guess is as good as mine dawg," Cool sighed, "'cause I damn sure don't know. Back in the day I know I wasn't as faithful, but who woulda ever thought that my infidelity would result in me getting shitted on after all these years."

"Dig that," Black commiserated.

"It's like the broad woke up one mornin' and decided to get herself a new niggah," Cool fumed; with a baffling expression on his mug. "It's typical, though." Black chuckled at his remark, as he continued. "You laughin' my niggah, but it's factual, ya dig?"

"I'm tripping' 'cause you wasn't gone but for a minute."

"Dig that," Cool agreed, "but statistics show that most women leave their beau when he's in a confined state. I just never thought it would be me... I mean, I thought we were fuckin' soul mates!"

"Don't sweat it, let it....shit happens" Black said encouragingly.

"Never that," Cool assured, as he continued. "I'll admit, I was fuc'd up at first, jus' keepin' it real, my niggah." But now, I'm finna live my life. Pimp hoes, slammin' Lexus and Mercedes Benz doors." They both chuckled at his street terminology. "I ain't gon' hate, though, I wish the broad well, besides, this new niggah may have somethin' more to offer her," he stressed optimistically.

"Yeah, but I wouldn't bank on that my niggah," Black grimaced, " I mean, ya know her an' Shawana still talk, right?"

"I know they tight," Cool replied.

"Well, Shawana's job had a party, and she invited them, that's where I seen the busta at."

"Whaaat?" Cool uttered comically.

"Yes suh," Black chuckled, "they were in Trina's car an' e'erythang... Big chunky lookin' broke fucka if you ask me."

"No shit?!" Cool grinned.

"Jus' callin' it like I see it, ya dig?" Black smirked.

"So, she jumped out a limo into a pinto, huh?" Cool ridiculed metaphorically; taking another sip of his drink.

"I suppose dawg, it appears that way to me," Black chuckled, as they both shook their heads in a perplexed state of mind.

Cool pondered briefly; taking another swig of his drink. He figured his former girlfriend got the prudish type of guy she always wanted. Maybe he was too street oriented for her, he thought. But somewhere along the line, he had a gut feeling she would truly regret ever leaving him.

CS

As Cool took the exit off of Interstate 59, almost to his destination, he contemplated all the necessary moves he must make tomorrow. Such as, dropping by the mall to cop some more up to date gear. He also planned to give his mother some cash; on general purposes. Plus, stash a thousand dollars weekly in her closet; for legitimate business reasons. He had come up with an array of business concepts while in servitude, and aimed to implement them once his finances were in order.

Pulling in the dilapidated apartment complex browsing for the correct unit, he cursed vehemently out loud to himself; as he endured a rough ride on the raggedy parking lot pavement. As he got out the car to knock on the door, he couldn't believe how tranquil the surroundings were. Normally, cats be loitering around getting high waiting in line for a haircut. Matter-of-fact, he was expecting to get a trim while there, himself, but the apartment looked vacant, he thought, as he knocked on the door anyway.

"Hey there, ya finally made it on in, eh?" Angel's dad greeted; with a southern accent.

"Believe that," Cool smiled; shaking the man's hand, as he continued. "Is Angel around?"

"Naw. I don't think she comin' through here t'day. She stay over there off Broadway wit' her momma now. Ain't nobody here but me an' Lil' Red," Mr. Wright informed.

"They left y'all home alone, huh?" Cool chuckled.

"Yuh. Come on in, I give ya her phone number," Mr. Wright invited, as Cool followed him inside.

"I see them sons of yours ain't aroun', I sure wanted to get me a fade. You think they'll be back anytime soon?" Cool asked.

"Ya know how they are, they ain't changed," Mr. Wright indicated, grinning, "they probably be back soon, though. I know they aroun' here somewhere. Have a seat Carlos, let me find a pen so I can write this girl number down for ya," he said, as he disappeared to the back.

Lil' Red emerged out the back room, curious to know who his grandfather was conversing with.

"What's up Lil' Red?" Cool spoke; grinning at the identical look the boy has of his deceased father.

"Hey," Lil' Red uttered nonchalantly; oblivious to who he was speaking to.

"You don't remember me man?" Cool asked knowingly, as he chuckled at Lil' Red shaking his head no.

"Boy you done forgot who Carlos is?" Mr. Wright intervened, as he reappeared. Lil' Red shook his head again speechless, displaying the same characteristics of his late father – tacit and insidious. "It's been awhile since he seen ya Carlos. Here the number, she oughta be home, 'cause she gotta work in the mo' nin'," he grinned informatively; handing the number to Cool.

"Thanks, I'll try to call her tonight," Cool replied, as he continued. "Tell them boys of yours I be back tomorro' to get me a cut. I'ma head on back to the Southside... I see ya later Lil' Red," he diverted toward the boy, as he strolled toward the door.

"Bye Carlos," Lil' Red responded bashfully.

"I see y'all tomorro' Mr. Wright," Cool said; chuckling at the boy's reaction; concurrently reaching in his pocket trying not to reveal his whole wad. "Here ya go little homie," he uttered; handing Lil' Red a hundred dollar bill.

"Whatcha say boy," Mr. Wright grinned; gazing in Lil' Red direction.

"Thank ya!" Lil' Red beamed gratefully.

"We see ya later Carlos," Mr. Wright said with a smile.

"Ah'ight," Cool chuckled, as he walked out the door.

As Cool cruised along, he ran into Slim and Boo walking down the street; with an inebriated look on both their mugs. He made a futile attempt to get one of them to cut him a tight bald fade. They both rejected the task until tomorrow, because they were not yet finished indulging in the mass amount of drugs and alcohol they consumed daily. A damn shame of wasted talent, he thought, as he sped off shaking his head in ridicule. The hair industry was definitely a lucrative field Cool wanted to pursue, but he knew he couldn't succeed in the hair arena with employees such as Slim and Boo. "Oh well," he thought aloud, as he dialed Angel's number on his homie's cellular phone. The phone rung several times before she finally answered with a cranky tone.

"Hello," Angel muttered.

"Hello... Angel," Cool replied skeptically.

"This she. Who's this?" Angel asked vaguely.

"It's Carlos," he assured, "I didn't mean to wake you... How you doin'?"

"I'm okay," Angel yawned, "I just gotta work in the mornin'."

"I understand, I just wanted to rap to you 'bout a few matters. I guess I'll try to catch up wit' cha sometime tomorrow, when you get off," Cool said sincerely.

"When they letcha out?" Angel asked; with a more vibrant tone now.

"The otha day," he informed.

"Em-hm. Do you still remember where I work?" she insured.

"I think so," he hesitated. "You talkin'-'bout over there in the ol' 'hood right?"

"Yes. You can come visit me there any time before six tomorrow. Jus' come to the las' suite in the buildin', Dr. Mosley's office," she explained.

"Done deal. I'll try to make it before six... I jus' left your dad's crib, that's how I discovered your whereabouts. Ya know that little niggah Red done forgot who I was," he huffed with a chuckle.

"It's been so long since he seen ya, hell. What he do, look atcha crazy?" she laughed.

"Yeah, until I slipped him a C-note. I think now he wanna be my friend," he said, as they both laughed at his comment. "Well, I'ma letcha get some rest, I don't wantcha to be late for work, an' blame it on me."

"I'll be alright, but that's not a bad idea," she replied drowsily, as she continued. "Let me give you my pager number in case you don't make it."

After she gave him the number, they both said their goodbyes. He then phoned Renee´ to see if she was game for some freaking. Which she welcomed; anticipating his arrival. He arrived shortly, because he was already in the vicinity. She was so enthused to see him, she eagerly led him to her chambers, where they fucked like dogs in heat. Since he never ate pussy before, he decided to give it a go. She was totally in awe by the downtown maneuvering of his tongue, as she gripped the sheets moaning his name with delight, while he lapped her clitoris rhythmically with his tongue; like a dog taking a much needed water break. Simultaneously finger fucking her with his two longest fingers. He didn't appear to be a novice thanks to his homie Blue from the joint and his astuteness to remember all the specifics of his homie's pussy eating tales. The stories were so fascinating, that cunt eating became one of his short-term goals. He dubbed this as another alluring tactic he could use, to manipulate all the females of his choice; making them all kowtow to his demands. Luckily for Renee´, he needed to get his practice on.

Once their prior vulgar engagement culminated in self-satisfaction, Cool decided to get him some rest. He expected tomorrow's schedule to be hectic; due to his need for more clientele; and his determination to get it.

Chapter-7

A t 10:00 a.m., Cool opened his eyes to find Renee´ sound asleep; with her succulent ass resting against his leg. This gave him an erecton ; prompting him to give her a rude – but pleasant – awakening; by forcing his stiff penis in her uncovered twat from the rear. She wasn't as sleepy as he thought, because she willingly parted her thighs just enough for his manhood to enter her. He grinned diabolically as he rolled her over on her stomach, and penetrated fiercely. His testes slammed hard against her, as they both groaned with ecstasy; perspiring from the writhing movement of both their bodies, as she frantically threw her pussy back at him. He couldn't bear the tantalizing sensation any further as he shot his steamy juices in her intimate abyss.

After his eruption, he kissed her tenderly on the back of her neck. Then, hopped up to go take a shower.

"Baby what time is it?" Cool asked, as he stretched; displaying his rock hard penis.

"It's 10:30, baby," Renee´ cooed, as she eyed the wristwatch that lay loosely on her end table. "Boy you sure know how to make me feel good," she stressed giddily.

"What time the mall usually open?" he asked; smiling at the look of contentment on her face.

"Aroun' ten or eleven, I think," she replied with a vague expression, "Ooh I wanna go," she requested.

"I ain't goin' yet baby girl, it'll be later on, I got otha moves to make," he down-played; knowing he was headed there as soon as he left her place.

He needed a few new threads, and was not trying to do no tricking. He knew he must stick to his objective: make all females pay him; not the other way around.

"You don't ever wanna take me nowhere," she carped. "You make me sick!"

"Don't be like that baby girl," he consoled, as he kissed her on the forehead. He took a hundred dollar bill from his pants and handed it to her. "When I decide to go to the mall, I'ma let cha know, ah'ight?" he lied.

"Yuh right, you'll tell me any damn thang to shut me up!" she bickered.

"Chill baby," he sighed, "e'erythang kool-aid," he grinned on the sly, as he strolled to the lavatory to get spruced up.

She knew she wasn't going to see his face again, until he was ready to get it on. She followed behind him like the pied piper to the shower.

She grabbed a washcloth and did the honors of washing his body. Then she dropped down to her knees looking up at him with a devious grin, as she stroked his dick with the soapy washcloth gently. His flaccid rod instantly stood at attention, as he glanced down admiring how sexy she looked with the water glistening off her face and silky hair. His legs began to tremble as she deep throated his love stick; until he shot his load between her luscious lips.

"You not suppose to spit my vanilla shake out baby," Cool quipped; laughing at her rinse his sperm out of her mouth.

"Hm," Renee´ sputtered, laughing at his antics, "I can't swallow all that baby."

"Sure you can, it's good for you," he replied jokingly, as he got out the tub to put on his clothes.

"Whatevah niggah!" she grinned, as she bathed herself.

By the time she finished, he was already dressed about to brush his teeth with a new toothbrush she gave him. Once he finished, he headed toward the door ready to take on the world, as she followed suit, pouting like a brat, because he was leaving.

CS

Driving around in search of a parking space at the crowded Sharpstown Mall, Cool began to think about his homie D.J. who he was locked up with. He knew he could reap monetary rewards from the bumpkins in his homie's small city. That's why his aim was to set up shop with D.J.'s assistance. He vowed to give D.J. a call as soon as he went to his mom's house.

As Cool strolled inside the mall, zeal sparked in his eyes from the vast amount of honeys sashaying all over the place. He couldn't resist testing his fly rhetoric on a couple of dime pieces that crossed his path. Both of them were intrigued by his proposal; allowing him to have their phone numbers.

After he finished conversing with the females, he entered a store called Georgio's. Their selection of leathers, minks, alligators, and silks fitted the criteria of all pimps, playas, and hustlers. He was greeted cordially by one of the most seductive looking foreign ladies life has to offer. Eye candy at it's finest, he thought, as he glanced at his main man George smiling in the background.

"What's up my man, long time no see?" George greeted with an Italian accent; formally shaking Cool's hand..

"I've been ina world far from here my friend, but I'm back now," Cool replied mysteriously, as they both chuckled. "How's business my friend?"

"Business is great, especially since you've showed up Carlos. I got some new stuff in man… Check this out," George responded, with a sales pitch, as they both strolled toward the suits and assorted color alligator footwear. "You like? Because you know I'll take good care of you my man," he assured.

"Ya know I know that," Cool smirked; observing the Coogi shirts with matching alligator sandals George laid out for him to view. "Yeah that's nice, but I need an outfit to wear out. Think you can oblige?"

"No problem. I'll get my tailor to measure you, we'll have you rolling in about thirty minutes. Is that quick enough for you?" George asserted.

"Fa sure. Soun' like a plan to me," Cool replied pleasingly.

Between George and his stunning employee, Cool walked out the store cleaner than a clap doctor with three additional hook ups. He never imaged shelling out twenty-five hundred, but George made him an offer he couldn't refuse.

CS

Pulling in front of his mom's house, he noticed her heading out somewhere. She scrutinized his approach backing out the driveway, and paused to see if he wanted something.

"Roll down the window Ms. Thang!" Cool joked.

"I'll be right back," Ms. Hudson informed, " I'm jus' going to the grocery store right quick."

"I wanted to give ya this, jus' in case I don't be here when you get back," Cool said; handing her five hundred dollars he pulled out from his pocket.

"Thank ya. I see you done bought yourself some new clothes. Where mine at?" Ms. Hudson smirked.

"Shh," Cool gruffed giddily, "you got five bills baby go buy ya somethin' nice, that's why I gave it to you... Where you put my stuff Trina brought over here the otha day?"

"Look there on the porch, under them sheets," Ms. Hudson replied, " let me go, I'll be back "

Cool went in the house to put away his new apparel, as well as scour through the possessions he left behind with his former girlfriend.

Rambling through the well-packed boxes, Cool stumbled upon what he was searching for. He was thrilled to see his 9 mm glock; with crimson trace infrared laser beam built inside, still in mint condition. He knew leaving his property with Trina deemed the best move if he still wanted it when he got out.

He now looked through his penitentiary data for his homie D.J. phone number. Once he located it, he dialed vehemently, because his intuitions signaled signs of wealth in the making.

"Hello is Doug home?" Cool asked the female, who answered the phone politely.

She put him on hold, as he heard her bellowing his homie's moniker in the distance.

"Hello... Who this is?" D.J. asked with a country drawl.

"Wha'd up niggah, you can't greet a niggah better than that?" Cool snapped.

"Whoevah this is need to tell me before I hang this mu'fucka up, ya dig?" D.J. fumed.

"Calm ya ass down, this Carlos damn fool!" Cool chuckled.

"Where I know you from playboy?" D.J. asked dubiously.

"Damn niggah, it ain't been that long since I seen you! It's Cool damn fool!" Cool ridiculed.

"Oh shit! What's up baby boy, when you get out?!" D.J. recollected excitedly.

"I been home for a couple of days now," Cool replied. "How soon can you make it down? I got a proposition for ya?"

"Tomorro' at the latest kinfolk," D.J. gasped, "I got a couple of irons in the fire I need to tend to firs'."

"Ah'ight niggah , don't fuck aroun' and miss the boat, know-wha'-I'm-talkin'-'bout?' Cool coerced on the sly.

"If I could come t'day my niggah I would, I ain't gon' front, 'cause I know you 'bout business, jus' bare wit' me dawg," D.J. expressed with integrity.

"Ah'ight niggah," Cool chuckled, as he continued. "So how in the hell did you forget about a niggah so quick? We all thought your ass was gon' drop a kite. Wha'd up wit' that?"

"I ain't forget, I jus' been tryna get my shit together, it's hectic out here, ya-feel-me?" D.J. sighed.

"Dig that," Cool agreed. "Sounds like to me you need to get on down here ASAP then, my frien'," he suggested. "So what have you been doin' for the past few months?"

"Tryna keep my head above water wit' my landscapin' occupation." D.J. clued.

Deciphering his figure of speech, Cool knew he was talking about selling marijuana. They practiced being impeccable with their street vernacular while in the joint.

"I feel ya D baby, I'ma help you broaden your horizons a bit. It's like that on my end, so the sooner I see yo' face, the less time we gotta waste," Cool expressed rhythmically, as they both chuckled.

"I feel ya o' fly ass niggah, D.J. grinned, "tomorrow a done deal fa sure."

"Ah'ight then, I'ma be lookin' for you now. I ain't jus' trippin', but I'm on a mission, know-wha'-I'm-talkin'-'bout?" Cool alerted.

"I dig fool," D.J. confessed.

They hung up, vowing to rendezvous sometime tomorrow. Cool knew D.J. never experienced the action he was about to bestow on him, but Cool's judgment led him into giving certain individuals golden opportunities.

CS

At 1:00 pm Money finally decided to get off his derriere´ and see about his vehicle being worked on. As he dragged toward the lavatory to spruce up, he read the short note taped to the vanity mirror. The family went to his father-in-law's house for a fish fry. He was not that chummy with his wife's father. Probably why she didn't bother to wake him, he thought. Still a little unkempt, he strolled to the kitchen to fix himself a glass of orange juice, concurrently dialing Terry's shop number on a cordless phone.

"Terry's car audio," a voice greeted.

"Is Terry in?" Money replied.

"Yes. Hold for one moment please," the receptionist said; putting him on hold.

Money laughed at the country tunes that jutted out the receiver.

"Hello," Terry spoke; taking Money out of his cheerful thoughts.

"What's up o' honeycomb head ass niggah?" Money joked. "You can't find no better music to play on your machine man?"

"Aw hell," Terry sighed. "What do you want? Don't tell me you calling about that bucket?"

"Damn right!" Money fumed. "Bet you ain't even started on my shit, huh?"

"I been through with that thing," Terry quipped, "you need to come get it, because it's taking up space."

"Ah'ight o' buildin' wrecker head mu'fucka," Money jeered, as they cackled hanging up.

Once Money dressed, he rolled a cigar size blunt, dipped it in some syrup, and phoned Cool to pick him up. He fired up the sticky treat, while awaiting his homie's arrival.

CS

As Cool cruised down Money's street, he phoned him informing that he was near. He laughed at the chinky look in Money's eyes, as they rode on their way to Page-Net (beeper store).

It only took a brief moment to obtain a pager. They were pulling in Terry's shop parking lot twenty minutes later.

As they got out of the car, Cool was dazzled by all the customized vehicles scattered about.

"Damn! That big head niggah still got it," Cool announced, as he observed the manufactured way T.V. monitors were mounted in the back of the head-rests of a Chevy Suburban.

"Yeah," Money agreed, "that wagon wheel head basta'd know his shit."

They chuckled mutually.

Terry spotted them and emerged with safety glasses hanging from his neck.

"What's up guys?" Terry greeted; sounding like a yuppie, as he continued. "Well if it ain't old Carlos."

"That's Mr. Carlos to you nig'... I mean white boy," Cool snapped comically, as they all broke out in a laughing hysteria.

Terry displayed the middle finger toward Cool offensively. They teased him, because he was one of those Caucasian sounding Negros with a white wife.

"I hope my shit sounds as good as it looks," Money said as he analyzed the installment job in his ride.

"Ain't nothing but one way of finding that out knuckle head. Look on the wall, your keys should be hanging up there," Terry replied cynically; pointing in the direction of the keys, as he continued. "Hop in Carlos, I want you to hear this, so you can bring me some of your money too," he beamed with confidence.

Terry turned on the system and began to delineate the instructions on how to operate the VCR, E.Q., and the head unit that controlled the two T.V. monitors that were meticulously mounted in the sun visors. They all agreed jovially that the clarity was superb. Both agreed and lauded Terry for a job well done. Although Money's MPV van looked plain jane, the interior assured the symbolic meaning of a baller's ride.

They all went inside. Money complained along the way, but didn't mine paying the abundant bill. He got hooked up like he wanted, so he felt a nice gratuity was in order.

After they finished inside, Cool and Money strolled out to the parking lot; leaving Terry behind to count all the bills for services rendered.

CS

Since there were no patients to tend to, Angel surfed the web until one of her counterparts informed her of a visitor waiting. She paused curiously to see who it was, as she sashayed toward the waiting area.

"What's up Carlos?" Angel greeted.

"I'm good, an' ya-self?' Cool responded with a smile.

"I'm fine," Angel assured, "come on back we can talk in the lounge area," she suggested.

He followed her to the back. As they strolled along, Cool detected the stares. He admired the attention and took it as a form of admiration that his appearance was grand instead of insipid.

"I see you done got slim an' trim while in there," Angel began, as they seated on the sofa.

"Yeah, I partook ina a few physical activities," Cool replied modestly. "So, what happened to my dawg?" he transitioned topics seriously.

"I guess it was just his fate," Angel sighed, "but he got out there bad after you went away ... we didn't even fool aroun' any more"

"No shit!" Cool replied, stunned.

"Yep," Angel said; shaking her head in disbelief. "He started stealin' money out of my purse, smoking that dip, an' drankin' that syrup shit. I tried to help him, but you already know how stubborn he is. Everybody an' they mama hook'd on that codeine and PCP shit nowadays," she chuckled. "I tol' him that shit wasn't cute, especially that codeine, that shit ain't nothing but liquid heroin."

"Yuh I know," Cool flustered. "That shits addictive too, ain't it?"

"Like crack, but fools don't realize. It's the latest craze, though," Angel smirked, as she continued. "It would kill me to hear him say, that what he was doin', was the way playas did it. I'm like, yeah right, retarded playas."

They both chuckled.

"Shit I ain't trippin', I'll stick to my liquor," Cool assured.

She went on degrading his cousin for awhile. She even brought up the Screw tapes that urged people to go out and purchase PCP dipped weed, along with codeine mixed with soda, in order to feel the slow tempo music his tapes produced. Cool knew his cousin was a little audacious, but never imagined him being a threat to society. Judging Angel's depiction, the calamity of his cousin was bound to happen.

"Well enough about that," Angel finalized. "How's it going wit' you?"

"I'm straight, can't complain too much, know-wha'-I'm-talkin'-'bout?" Cool gestured.

"I heard that... You know Lil' Red birthday tomorrow, looks like he got his present from you early," Angel said.

"That's nothin', if you got time tomorrow, we'll go get him somethin' better, besides, he probably done spent that hun'ed by now," Cool assumed jokingly.

"I doubt it, that little niggah be savin', but I ain't doin' nothin' tomorrow, so it's whatever," Angel insisted.

"Well, it's settled then. One mo' thang...." Cool paused; gathering his thoughts. "I'm lacking in communications, somethin' I desperately need, 'cause pullin' up to them pay phones could be hazardous to ones health, know-wha'-I'm-talkin'-'bout?"

They both snickered.

Reading between the lines, she deciphered exactly what he was getting at.

"So, you want me to get you a phone, huh?" Angel smirked knowingly.

"How you know?" Cool replied surprised.

"Duh," Angel lampooned," it doesn't take a brain surgeon niggah."

"Well, you figured me out," Cool replied.

"I think I can do a little somethin'-somthin' for ya," Angel assured.

"You a lifesaver," Cool thanked with a grin, "you just removed one of my hurdles."

"I'll pick you up one when I get off. Houston Cellular should still be open, but it's gon' cost you now," Angel quipped playfully.

"I ain't got no qualm wit' that," Cool replied; pulling five hundred dollars out of his pocket, passing it to her.

"I was jus' joshin'," Angel atoned, handing back half the money. "I don't need but two fifty, that should cover it." "kno'-wha'-I'm talkin'-'bout?" She mimicked as they laughed.

She walked him to his car. On his way out, he waved goodbye to her gawking co-workers, as they all waved back with euphoric expressions on their faces.

Betrayal of Peers

Chapter – 8

Approaching Chicago's house, Cool smiled at the big body Lexus – with twenty inch chrome Brabus Blade rims – parked in his homie's yard. Judging the scenery, Cool figured his homie was still up to his dastardly, money-making deeds. As he got out walking toward the house, he noticed the garage door raising up.

"What's goin' down Cool?" Chicago greeted; giving him some dap. "I heard you was out."

"Yuh, I'm back baby boy, looking for action, know-wha'-I'm-talkin'-'bout?" Cool hinted, as he continued. "I see ya still handlin' up, from the looks of e'erythang."

"It's all good. I still dabble a little, but I got some eighteen-wheelers too now," Chicago boasted proudly. "What's the deal, ya back on the block or what?"

"Thought you knew," Cool retorted, "set back for a major come back."

They both chuckled as Chicago's wife intervened. She stepped out the house fraternizing; on her way to the market.

"Hey Cool, you made it back to us, huh?" she spoke knowingly.

"Back in the flesh. How you been doin'?" Cool spoke back.

"I'm fine," she assured, "that place sure know's how to preserve you, you look good man," she commented; observing his revamped physique.

Cool merely blushed at her statement, while Chicago laughed. He was never jealous of his wife's friendliness toward his true homeboys.

"Yeah, working out was one of my past times, I guess it paid off a little," Cool said coyly.

"Well, it sure did," she agreed, as she switched topics. "Chi' baby move your car so I can get out, I'm off to the flea market."

"You have fun at the flea market!" Cool announced.

"Yuh she sure will, spendin' my damn money," Chicago mumbled in a low tone; causing Cool to chuckle, as he let his wife out. As he got back out the car, they continued their tête-à-tête. "So, Cool, like I was sayin', what they hit for?"

"Tell ya what dawg, I'ma keep it real wit'cha, I'ma try to meet or beat your price. I ain't tryna make no killin', know-wha'-I'm-talkin'-'bout? Pull my coat to what you normally pay, an' I'll see what I can do, ya dig?" Cool spoke like a true salesman.

Baiting him in deemed the most profitable way of handling the matter, Cool thought. Then, voila! You up the ante.

"Tell ya what Cool, since you put it that way, the las' one I sco'ed I paid sixteen," Chicago slightly fabricated; in hopes of a deal. "If ya price tight, I'll do somethin' wit'cha ina hour."

"Since we go back kinfolk, I'll do you one fi'ty eight all day, e'eryday, that gives me the leeway of a couple hun'ed. You my niggah, so I'm basically doin' it on the strength."

"Sound good to me. Look here, I wantcha to come back ina hour. Will you do a half too?" Chicago remarked contentedly.

"I thought you knew. Half, quarter, half of a quarter, zone, shhh, jus' call me ya humble servant," Cool retorted with candor.

"Man, you still a fool I see," Chicago chuckled.

Cool was elated to have added another soldier to his roster; in order to meet his financial goals. Now, he must maintain their satisfaction to meet his quota, he thought. Knowing the dope game wasn't the proper way to claim fame. That's why his original plan was to get it while the getting was good; go legit; and get out before he got caught.

CS

Black was just leaving his new house. Leaving his wife and kids behind to get acquainted with their new surroundings, while he and the movers traveled back to his old house to gather a few more items. As he drove along, his cellular phone began to ring.

"Hello," Black greeted.

"What's the deal Bliz-zack!" Cool spoke with a distinctive street vernacular.

"Tryna move some of this shit," Black complained.

"Still fuckin' wit' that, huh?" Cool snickered.

"Yuh-yuh. What's on ya mind dawg?' Black responded.

"Let me find out you a mind reader," Cool bantered, as they both chuckled. "You got time to meet me at the spot.... I got to get my serve on."

"I see you keepin' busy playa. I'm headin' that way now, gimme twenty minutes," Black assured.

"Bet," Cool replied; hanging up the phone abruptly.

Since he had a little time to kill, Cool decided to stop by his cousin's house. Pondering his cousin's hustling abilities, made him smile; knowing he would play a prosperous role within the faction.

CS

The mother of the house screamed at her kids, using cusswords as if they were adults. Even though she just scolded all of them, she still demanded them to stop bawling, and clean up the mixture of confetti and clothes, scattered about the unkempt house. The daddy of the house was knocked out in the master bedroom. Their whole household was ghetto ridden. Big Lou sold drugs during the wee hours, while his trifling wife lounged around living ghetto fabulous off of his dough. Her promiscuity made her the talk of the town. Truth be told, when Big Lou was doing a county bid, she was so promiscuous she conceived a child by his former best friend. Nevertheless, he still loves her. He helped raise two kids, and the other two kids that weren't his. He even took care of his wife's mother-in-law, and her two kids for that matter. Since they all lived under the same roof, he felt obligated to provide for everyone. The outlandish way they all lived, they could easily be dubbed; The Addam's Family.

While Big Lou's wife continued to bellow at her kids, there was a knock at the door.

"Who the hell knockin' at my door?!" Dee-Dee, Big Lou's wife shouted, as she peered out the window noticing who it was.

"It's your kinfolk crazy ass, open the damn door!" Cool roared back.

"Ain't nobody home, go away!"

Giggling at her own antics, she finally gave in and let Cool in. The kids all stared him down, as he entered the living room greeting the little ones endearingly. Simultaneously, talking trash to Dee-Dee, as he strolled toward the master bedroom. He chuckled within, because he could hear his cousin snoring in the distance.

"Lou baby wake up!" Cool disturbed; shaking him to no avail.

"Get out the way! I bet I can get his fat ass up!" Dee-Dee sneered.

Cool chuckled, pondering the old adage: the pot calling the kettle black, because she is just as rotund as his cousin is. Cool moved aside; roaring with laughter, as she flailed her hand with force across his immense sized tush.

"Get up Lou, ya cousin here!" Dee-Dee barked; mission accomplished.

"Girl!" Big Lou hissed; with slobber leaking out the corner of his mouth. "You musta bumped yo' fuckin' head!"

They laughed at his irate nature.

"If it wasn't your kinfolk, I wouldn't have bothered you," Dee-Dee explained remorsefully.

"Hol' up," Cool began chucklingly. "You don't wanna holla at cha peeps ?!"

"Cooly, wha'd up baby?!" Big Lou responded; wiping the matter from his eyes; regaining awareness.

They carried on embracing like they haven't seen each other in a couple of decades, while Dee-Dee grimaced enviously; leering at the profound unconditional love they have for each other.

"How touchin'," Dee-Dee sneered comically.

They both paused tacitly; blasé toward her remark.

"Any way, my niggah," Cool continued, "I got out a couple of days ago."

"Why you didn't holla kinfolk. You don't love me no mo'?" Big Lou teased.

"I had a few co'ners to bend, matters to tend to, know-wha'-I'm-talkin'-'bout? Don't get it twisted, you know me an' you like two plus two," Cool replied with cadence, as they chuckled; giving each other dap.

"I see you lookin' like a million bucks niggah," Big Lou observed.

"You know how I do," Cool bragged, "we'll all be fly before long. I see you still layin' on your ass, musta been up all night ?"

"Ain't a damn thang change Cooly, you don't work, you don't eat, simple as that."

"Dig that," Cool grinned knowingly. "So what's been crackin'?"

"Oh, it's goin' down, I jus' been havin' to deal wit' these cake ass niggahs since you been gone, crazy ass shit."

"Dig that. It's all good now, goddamn-me... Get some rest, I gotta hit this stang, but when I come back, I'ma brang you somethin'. You still like it hard, huh?" Cool uttered assumingly.

"No doubt," Big Lou stressed, "I still ain't learnt how to cook that shit yet dawg."

"Ain't no thang, I gotcha," Cool assured.

Cool cracked up at his cousin's comment, as they entered the living room to witness Dee-Dee still bickering at the kids. Cool waved bye to the kids with an expression of pity, because their mother was being a cruel bitch. After he left the madhouse, he headed to Black's house to pick up and make a delivery.

CS

The movers were placing boxes in the truck, while Black stood supervising; making sure they loaded the cargo right. He received a call from Money; stating he was on his way to drop off some cash he owed. Just as they walked back outside to take another load, Cool pulled up. Black grinned knowingly, as he approached.

"What's the deal?" Cool responded.

They strolled in the house leaving the movers outside tending to the box arrangements in the truck.

"So, Cool baby, whatcha need?" Black asked curiously.

"The last two you got my niggah, but I need a half bird hard, so I need to jump in the lab for a minute, ya dig? I jus' left Big Lou's crib. I'ma put him down wit' a little, plus my nig' Chicago want a brick an' a half."

"Shit! Soun' like I need to get on the horn and place anotha order to fat ass!" Black said, as they both chuckled. "You been putting in work kinfolk. When I leave to drop off anotha load, you can shake an' bake then. You still know how to get down, huh?"

"Niggah please! Ask no stupid ass questions, and I won't tell you no stupid ass lies," Cool shot back, "it's my profession dawg, and ones' specialty always remain imbeded in the brain," he assured, as they both chuckled.

"Dig that," Black continued, "I was jus' makin' sure, niggah." You shouldn't need no mo' than an hour an' thirty, so I'll stay away 'til then. The keys to the hoop' over there on the desk along with the dope," he assured. "When they finish loadin' up out there, I'ma bounce. Money supposed to stop by and drop off some change he owe. Tell that niggah he gon' have to wait on his shit, 'cause we out 'til later on."

"Say kinfolk," Cool began cautiously. "You think it's kosher to keep evidence out like that?"

"Naw, I usually keep that shit put up, but I took it out the stash, 'cause I was gon' bake later on. I try to keep some hard shit ready, but your ass been movin' the shit like abracadabra," Black expressed comically, "which, is all good ." They both chuckled at his axiom. "But next time, I'ma get ten of them mu'fuckas, since you puttin' it down like that. Then, we'll cook three off top, 'cause I got niggahs like Dave, for example, be wantin' it already ready too."

"Dig that," Cool continues with a grimace. "You still servin' that retard?"

"Damn right!" Black informed. "His money green, an' it spen' the same like e'erybody else's, feel me?"

"No doubt," Cool agreed, "but I hate dealin' wit' that whole looney ass family of his, know-wha'-I'm-talkin'-'bout?" They both chuckled knowingly. "I'll probably get Money or Ray to shoot over there when he get ready. Them mu'fuckas screws loose for real," he emphasized, as he continued. "That niggah be still cursin' an' fightin' his T-Jones an' sistah?"

"Hell yuh," Black chuckled, "an' they still be dippin' in that niggah stash too."

"I'll probably go through there to trip off they silly asses, it's been a while since I seen 'em," Cool chuckled also, "but I ain't makin' no habit of it, though. I'd rather pay Ray, he'll be glad to."

They continued chuckling in agreement.

On that note, Cool situated the product, grabbed the keys to the hooptie, and burnt off to serve his patron Chicago.

By the time he made it back, Money was there; on his way out the door to go drain some cash from his dope traps. He gave Cool some dap, as he got in his vehicle. Judging the bulky bag Cool possessed, Money knew Cool was progressing.

As Black trailed behind the movers to go drop off another load to his new pad, he phoned the connection; placing an order for ten kilos of coke. He was assured that Jim would pick up and drop off at approximately 8:30 p.m. He needed to be on standby, so the runner wouldn't be waiting outside by his lonesome looking suspicious.

Betrayal of Peers

Chapter – 9

Preparing crack was never a complex task for someone that took pride, and enjoyed being a mad scientist – so to speak – like Cool did. He cooked dope like an old fashion mother would put together a scrumptious meal; on Easter Sunday. It took him about forty-five minutes to cook the cookie like ounces, and clean up the mess he made. Thanks to the excessive Pyrex jars, and the two microwaves ovens, he was now on his way to his cousin's house to deliver the goods.

He made it there in fifteen minutes. Since his cousin was still laying on his tired ass, Cool left the dope with his annoying wife to put up for him.

After the illicit business transaction, he headed back to Black's house to swap cars – being there were no more runs to make. Rolling down MLK Blvd., he pulled into an Exxon convenience store to get some ice to replenish his drink. As he got out of the car, a destitute looking kid approached wanting to pump his gas for cash. He wasn't purchasing gas, but gave the little boy five dollars anyway.

"Thank-ya mister," the boy said gratefully, accepting the bill.

"You welcome," Cool replied back. "Next time I'm here ya owe me one," he gestured; while the boy nodded his head in agreement, jovially fleeing the scene. Cool was joking, he has a soft spot for kids even though he didn't have any yet.

Mulling about another business prospect, Cool traveled to the Westside of Houston, in hopes of his old chum Alan being there to welcome him. There was time to kill before he had to meet Angel, he thought. He noticed Alan standing in his yard in the distance, and was surprised to see his homeboy dawdling around the house.

"What's up Cool?" Alan slurred; like he was mentally slow; however has good money- making sense.

"E'erythang kool-aid, my niggah," Cool replied; giving him dap, "I'm glad I caught you at the crib... So what's poppin'?"

"I been doin' it, you know me," Alan emphasized; with a slight dyslexic speech. "I'm glad to see ya back dawg, ya know I rather deal wit' you. Ya look like you been out for a while dawg," he observed Cool's dapper stance.

"I jus' raised the otha day, but ya know I don't waste no time kinfolk," Cool gloated, as they both chuckled.

"I feel ya. I jus' done somethin', but when I'm ready I'ma get it from you ah'ight?" Alan assured.

This was sweet music to Cool's ears, because he had accumulated another soldier. His bonafide character; plus reputation for keeping top grade product, lured people he dealt with to do business with him first and foremost.

CS

There were people hanging outside of Mr. Wright's apartment waiting patiently for a haircut. It's phenomenal how much clientele Angel's brothers accumulated. Especially since they never attended school nor had a barber's license. As Cool drove up, the traffic reminded him of a crack house. "Them niggahs couldn't sell crack 'cause they'd smoke it all," he whispered, as he got out the car and went inside. Everyone, with the exception of the people that knew him, glared and mean mugged, as if they were straight hating on his presence.

He warded off the envy with a Colgate smile – taking it with a grain of salt – as he noticed Angel stepping out the back room with a box in her hand.

"Here ya go Carlos," Angel began, "you have to read the instructions to learn how to operate everything," she assured. "I'll let you know when the bill come in, I sent it to my place."

"I'm sure you will," Cool joked, as they both chuckled. "Thankya very much. Now, I don't have to worry 'bout a stick up kid approachin' me at a phone booth," he joked seriously.

"Where Lil' Red at?", he asked.

"He on the otha side of the apartments playin' wit' his friends," Angel informed.

"Uh-hm. Well, I guess I'll try to get a damn haircut," Cool sighed; leering at the traffic. "Slim, how many ya got baby boy!" he screamed; nodding toward the barber station set up in the abandoned dining room.

"What's up Cool ?!" Slim smiled. "I didn't see you come in c..co..come here let me holla at cha," he stuttered; pausing briefly in someone's head.

Cool approached the makeshift barber area, giving Slim and Boo dap, as they giddily complemented him on his grandiose appearance. Slim conspicuously whispered in Cool's ear, that he was next. Knowing it was imperative to tend to VIP patrons first, since they compensated the best.

Once in the chair, he gave Cool a tight bald fade in minutes. Jabbering all the while but, nevertheless, he took care of his business with those clippers.

"'Preciate cha kinfolk," Cool began; gazing at his hairdo in a homemade hand held mirror. "You still got it," he complemented.

"A... A... Ain't gon' ever lose it," Slim stammered.

Cool paid him twenty bucks; way more than the five bucks they normally charged for a hook up. Slim shook his head satisfied, as Cool strolled off to say his goodbyes to Angel before he left.

"Well, I'm out," Cool began, upon his approach. "That boy ain't came back yet?" he asked; referring to her son.

"Naw, not yet," Angel replied, brushing the excess hair off his shirt. "I think I'ma have to go get him, 'cause I'm about ready to head out myself," she explained. "Don't forget about our date tomorrow," she uttered in a seductive tone.

"I won't forget. I think I'm takin' tomorrow off as well, unless my clients forbid," Cool replied; without realizing she was flirting. "See ya later."

"I'll see ya tomorrow," Angel cunningly replied as they went their separate ways.

Chapter – 10

IT had been quite awhile since Mrs. Wright separated from her husband. She was in the kitchen preparing herself something to eat, when Angel suddenly came through the door with Lil' Red clutched in her arms. Angel laid her son's tired body down in her bed, then stepped back to the front where her mother was to watch television. She's been living with her mother every since her baby daddy got killed.

"Momma what cha cookin?"! Angel asked in the distance, as she flopped down on the sofa; flipping through the channels with the remote.

"Some fish an' salad! Ya want some?!" Mrs. Wright replied.

"I'll have some salad, it's too late to be eating fried fish," Angel shot back grimacing.

"Suit yourself, don't matter to me, I'm hungry," Mrs. Wright responded.

"Mom do you remember Carlos?" Angel asked; switching topics.

"Who's that?" Mrs. Wright answered.

"Big Red cousin," Angel assured, "he jus got out the pen. I seen him today, he stop by my job."

"Oh yeah, I remember him," Mrs. Wright said, regaining familiarity. "What he want?" she pried further.

"Nothin' really, jus' stop by to say hello. He heard about what happen to his cousin, so I kinda filled him in on what went down," Angel explained.

For some strange reason she thought about Cool on her way home. She hadn't been with a man intimately in awhile, she pondered. But none of the men who made passes at her, fit her criteria.

Talking with her mom was something she did sporadically. Deeming it obvious to her mother why she was having this chat. Angel didn't think Cool would be interested in her, but if so, she wouldn't overlook it, because he is definitely her type.

"Hmm," Mrs. Wright mulled. "So you think that's the only reason he showed up at your job?"

"What cha mean by that?" Angel frowned.

"I think he's interested in you," Mrs. Wright pointed out with a grin. "If he keep comin' around, you'll know," she emphasized.

"I never thought about it that way," Angel replied with a mirthful expression.

She was enthused by her mother's reaction, hoping Cool did have some amorous emotions for her, but was to coy to admit it.

"Well, we will jus' see what the future bring," Mrs. Wright smirked knowingly. "I'ma put your salad in the 'frigerator, I'm goin' to my room."

"Thank you," Angel replied.

Fatigue snuck up on her; while trying to watch the "Love Boat" (a television sitcom). She stretched out on the sofa – opting not to eat the salad – and drifted off to sleep.

CS

There were all types of vehicles scattered about the small parking lot of the club, Cool noticed. He parked across the street at a vacant strip center; additional parking when the club is full to capacity. Pulling in a parking space, he pondered the numerous times he passed by the adult joint, but never took the initiative to see what went on inside. Probably because tricking went against his ethos, he thought.

Before he entered, he phoned his homies to see what the delay was on their arrival. They both assured him they were en route, so he strolled in, paid his cover charge, and cased the joint for a seat.

Even though the place was packed like sardines in a can, a half clad bar maid still managed to find him a table in a cozy little area with a view. Sipping on the watered down drink she fetched him, he observed the sleazy decorum; as well as a few frail and paunchy broads who paraded around the ghetto atmosphere. There was still some black voluptuous broads – dime pieces for that matter – that stole his attention in a lustful way.

"Hey baby, can I sit wit' you?" a black goddess with a symmetrical ass and perky boobs, inquired cordially upon her approach.

Cool paused in awe, gawking at her stunning frame, before he allowed her to sit. The barmaid stood at attention, waiting to see if he wanted to order more drinks; noticing his previous drink was damn near empty.

"It would be my pleasure for you to join me," Cool began. "Would you care for a thirs' quencher?"

"Sure!" his newly found company replied, as she gestured toward the barmaid. "Carol bring me a gin an' grapefruit juice."

"Yuh Carol," Cool ordered also, "bring me anotha Remy Martin, make it a double, an' tell kinfolk to go easy on the water this time." he joked seriously, as they all chuckled.

"Ooooh baby, that's my song. Want a dance?" the broad asked cunningly; once the barmaid sashayed away.

Cool grinned; recognizing her game. Even though she exposed herself like a grifter, he was there to have fun, so, he didn't knock the hustle. Besides, he figured she would payback later, in more ways than one.

"Ah'ight boo," Cool grinned charmingly, "I'll letcha accumulate some of my evil faces, but make it somethin' to remember, ya dig?"

"Not a problem," she asserted, "they don't call me Juicy for nothing". She divested her top revealing her succulent boobs. Like a professional, she climbed on top of him with her sensuous routine; arousing his libido instantly. The barmaid emerged back with their cocktails, patiently enjoying the show until they finished.

"I mus' say, that was a treat baby girl," Cool sighed with satisfaction; while the dancer and the barmaid cackled in unison; leering at the bulge in his pants.

"I tol' you baby boy, I always aim to please," Juicy cooed seductively. She cased the joint, making sure the coast was clear; then unzipped his zipper; commencing to stroke his rod, as if they were behind close doors. The barmaid aloofly obtained her pay plus tip, then strolled off to give them a little privacy. "Damn baby I sure like the feel of your massive dick," she muttered, as she continued to dry jerk his member inconspicuously.

"Emmm," Cool murmured excited, but stable. "Whatcha doin' when ya get off?"

"Probably comin' wit' you daddy," Juicy teased.

"Soun' like a plan to me baby girl, "Cool replied; breathing heavily.

Juicy smiled wickedly; jerking his dick even faster now. Even though he was a stranger, she had a good vibe he wasn't a cop. He slumped down in his chair relishing the pro massage his penis; while he imagined having a broad with such an aptitude on his dream team. She is definitely a candidate needed to help jump-start his pandering venture, he thought.

"Well-well, I see you done blend in niggah!" a boisterous voice intervened.

Cool jumped startled; but relaxed, once he looked up to see it was his homie Black with two broads lingering behind him. One of the broads was from Cool's coming home shindig, while the other one was an unknown.

"Yuh, I done got acquainted niggah," Cool began, "but from the looks of thangs you the one got it goin' on," he grinned lasciviously; waving at the tasteful broads that tailed behind his cohort. Skillfully he eased his erect member back into his pants. In an attempt to camouflage the freaky behavior that took place, before they showed up disturbing his groove.

Glancing at Juicy, Cool could tell she was distraught by the other broads' presence. Probably feared that the women were trying to intervene on her money making scheme, he thought. They all fetched chairs and joined in. Roxanne introduced her co-worker name Star to Cool, as the bitch that didn't show up for his coming home party. Causing everybody to laugh at her foul criticism. Except for Juicy, she detected the amorous attention Cool now had on Star.

"Bitch you need to go find ya own man, 'cause this one taken!" Juicy sneered enviously toward Star.

Everyone displayed a shocked look by her insecurity. She deserved the right to be worried, because Star was much more attractive, even though Juicy's body was more curvaceous. Before Star could reply, Cool intervened.

"Look out baby girl," Cool began with suave mannerism, "firs' of all I don't mean to soun' discouragin'." Everyone gazed attentively as he continued. "But I'm not spoken for, actually, I came here to have fun, as well as diversify my occupational status."

"Oh really," Juicy replied curiously.

"No doubt, an' I'm seekin' beautiful women such as ya-self. You see, we can't let our inner ugliness take control over our destinies. We have to all unite, an' reap the rewards that will benefit all of our accounts. So, if ya feel me, slide me ya digits, an' we can go deeper into it at a more appropriate time. For the time bein', I'ma get to know this young beauty also, know-wha'-I'm-talkin'-'bout?" Cool disclosed.

They were all mesmerized by his philosophy. While the broads were all spellbound, Black chuckled; knowing his homie was hoodwinking with top-flight game.

"Damn daddy!" Juicy praised. "I shoulda known by your appearance that you was on anotha level. My bad. I'm slippin'… I'ma give you my number, you make sure you call me," she emphasized, "Don't even sweat the tip for the dance, shit, this time it's on me, but I could use anotha drank, though," she said; causing them to chuckle.

"Don't worry baby girl, I gotcha, good lookin' for bein' so sweet," Cool conceded.

"I'ma go find Carol ass then, 'cause it look like y'all all need one!" Juicy announced, as she stood up.

Juicy kissed Cool on the cheek, as she promenaded in the midst of the traffic the club contained. If his rhetoric took the same effect on all bitches, he'll accumulate a nice little stable in no time, Cool pondered deviously.

"So, kinfolk, where the hell Money at?" Cool transitioned toward Black.

"Let me hit that niggah, he shoulda been here by now," Black uttered concerned, as he took his cellular phone out of his pocket.

"Well well now , speak of the damn devil!" Cool chuckled, spotting Money at the entrance. He then stood up bellowing his name from a distance. Money recognized, displayed his gold and diamond grill, and strolled in their direction. "Damn my niggah, I thought you wasn't gon' make it!" Cool shrieked, giving him dap once he approached.

"Yuh niggah, I was jus' 'bout to call you!" Black added.

"I had an additional run to make." Money explained as he continued. "How y'all lovely ladies doin'?" he greeted, as they all exchanged pleasantries. "Buy a niggah a drink Cool!"

"Don't fret kinfolk, the waitress on the way," Cool assured. His remark must've conjured up Juicy and Carol, because they both strolled up instantly after that. Juicy slid her number to Cool, while Carol took their drink orders. "Carol baby, ya gotta keep checkin' on us now," he stressed. "What's the matter, we don't tip good enough?"

"Naw baby boy, that ain't it," Carol clarified, "you been breakin' me off, I jus' been spreadin' my hustle."

They all chuckled at her truthful response.

"Well, I tell ya what," Cool began; handing her a fifty dollar bill, "you working for us tonight, so keep our glasses full, baby doll." She kissed Cool on the cheek, elated by his generosity, before she swished away. "Money!" he continued; grasping his homie's attention. "This Ms. Juicy, in case you didn't already know."

"Dig that. I seen her aroun', but we never got acquainted. Obliged to meet you baby girl," Money fraternized; kissing Juicy's hand.

"Likewise," Juicy blushed giddily.

"Look out baby doll, keep my kinfolk company, why don't cha," Cool suggested.

"Ain't no thang daddy," Juicy replied submissively, as she flopped down in Money's lap.

"Cool you somethin' else!" Roxanne blurted suddenly; admiring his persuasive style.

"Yuh, he move quick!" Star concurred, as she sat in Cool's lap.

Carol finally made it back with their drinks, while the broads engaged in a simultaneous trio of lap dances. Cool stole Star's mind like hypnotherapists overtaking the minds of their patients. She obeyed him so quickly, it wasn't a question now that he would begin monopolizing women. Since Star seemed more 'bout it, she was gradually winning the overall battle. But time will tell, he thought.

The fun lasted till the club closed. They all decided to continue the partying at an after hour speakeasy. Money's inebriate state wouldn't allow him to continue on, but since he was still in control, they allowed him to drive home alone. As they entered the parking lot about to leave, some cat drove up grasping Star's attention. He was said to be an old friend. She tried to sell Cool a lame story but he wasn't buying. She hopped in the stranger's car with explanations, so Cool invited Juicy to roll with him. And the four of them left Star behind.

CS

Entering the parking lot of a lavish hotel, located within the Galleria Mall, made Cool realize the initial plan had changed. He didn't mind, because he'd rather get more acquainted with Juicy; instead of dwelling in some illegal speakeasy. Black arranged for two adjoining suites over the phone before they arrived; just in case they wanted to play the switch game on the dames. Something they did sporadically in the past. Since Black frequented the hotel, he coerced the valet attendant to bring them up a cold bottle of Crystal champagne for the occasion. Once they entered one of the suites, they immediately indulged in the bubbly. After a few glasses, Black and Roxanne went to their room to get their freak on. It amused Cool how well armed with condoms Juicy was. Probably had impromptu sex all the time, he thought.

During the sexcapade, the moans and groans boisterously escaped the walls from each room.

Once the fuck fest simmered down, Cool laid in the bed staring at the ceiling. For some particular reason he thought about Star. Her alluring style turned him on, but if she was spoken for he vowed not to sweat it. Suddenly, Black stepped in his room fully dressed; snapping Cool out of his daydreaming thoughts.

"Look out dawg, I gotta bounce," Black distressed, "it's 4:30, I don't want daylight to catch my ass, ya feel me."

Cool chuckled knowingly, as he eased out of the bed trying not to awake Juicy – simultaneously slipping on his silk boxers that lay loosely on the floor. He teased his homie in a low tone.

"Wifey gon' beat that ass," Cool smirked, as he continued. "Don't tell her you was wit' me niggah, have her lookin' at me all crazy," he sneered.

"Fuck you niggah!" Black roared laughing.

"Gon' get ghost kinfolk, I'll get atcha later," Cool suggested sincerely, "you leavin' ya girl behind?" he asked.

"Yeah," I'm leavin' her, drop her off for me," Black replied.

"Ah'ight ," Cool continued comically, "now getcha ass outta here, so I can crash, an' befor wifey beat that ass."

Black speechlessly shot him the middle finger on the way out the door, while Cool climbed back in bed with one of his future female prospects.

Chapter – 11

S unday is a day for rest and relaxation for most people, but not for D.J., he was up early. Mostly, he preferred rolling alone on his excursions. But since his wheels were in the shop,his homie Spencer agreed to bring him to Houston to see what Cool had in store for him. He was in need of a financial boost; especially since his marijuana business was not sufficient enough. Beaumont was only an hour drive from Houston. Glancing at his watch, D.J. projected they would be in the big city at 9:00 a.m.

Once Spencer arrived, D.J. gave his wife a kiss, grabbed his personal sack of marijuana – being he was a chain blunt smoker – and headed out the door on his way to his destination.

CS

The time displayed on the clock was 8:10 a.m. when Cool rolled over awaking out of his slumber. While wiping the matter from his eyes, regaining his focus, he stared at the naked voluptuous ass that laid next to him. The beautiful sight caused his libido to race fiercely. He obliged his freaky desires with early morning copulation to start the day off. Cunningly, he slipped on a condom in an attempt to give his victim a delightful awakening. Obviously, his prey was willing, because she rolled over jovially accepting his manhood between her thighs. Once again it's on he thought, as he elevated her legs on his shoulder – in a missionary position –

stabbing her fuck hole rapidly until she screamed with delight. Being that the adjoining suite door was ajar, Roxanne bickered jokingly about the commotion.

"Damn a niggah can't get no sleep aroun' here!" Roxanne complained. "Bitch quit makin' so much noise, it don't feel that good!" she sneered.

Cool continued to dick her down, while his victim screamed louder than before; with the combination of pain and pleasure stimulating her body. As they were both simultaneously climaxing, Roxanne decided to stand in the doorway. Voyeuristically, she gaped at their nude glistening bodies performing like dogs in heat. Getting aroused; wishing Black was there to allay her sexual frustration.

After the stellar performance, Cool glanced back noticing Roxanne's presence, with a diabolical grin.

"Care to join in baby girl," Cool asked lecherously.

"Black ain't here," Roxanne retorted, "I don't fuck nobody else without his permission," she smirked. "But I can accommodate Juicy wit' her fine ass," she admitted licking her lips.

"What!" Cool bellowed. Before he could articulate, Roxanne divested the thong and bra she had on, and climbed into the sack with them – spreading Juicy's thighs as she commence to muff diving head first – lapping up the leftover nectar between her victim's legs. "Shit! This better than watchin' a flick!" he beamed; giving them room to perform.

After the female pussy eaters finally had their orgasms, they both collapsed on the bed; faces smeared with vaginal juices.

"Damn, that felt good," Juicy purred.

"I hope it was as good for y'all as it was for me... Shit!" Cool emphasized.

They chuckled at his risqué humor; while gazing at him stroke his rock hard member.

"Come here daddy an' let me take care of that," Juicy cooed with lust in her eyes.

"I'ma go take me a shower," Roxanne continued comically, "tear that pussy up Cool, I got it ready for ya!"

She strolled to the adjourning suite, while Cool humped Juicy doggy style. Once they finished their third sexual session, they took a shower together, then ordered themselves some breakfast from room service. While they all lounged around eating, Cool and Roxanne pagers' vibrated back to back.

"Damn Cool they lookin' for us,!" she humored, as they all laughed.

Since Cool was on the only available line in the room, Roxanne had to go next door to make her call. Juicy stared at Cool noticing how giddy he was on the phone. She was quickly growing attached to him by the minute. His suave style, plus greatness in bed, gave her enough reason to kow-tow to his theories, and become a loyal member of his soon to be faction of fillies. The reason Cool was so elated on the phone was because his penitentiary homie was in town. He gave D.J. the directions to his mom's house.

"When ya get there kinfolk, jus' sit tight...," Cool said. "Gimme 'bout an hour..." "I'ma make it worth ya while..." "I gotta drop a couple of honeys off firs'..." "Okay." "Ah'ight later," he hung up.

As he continued his breakfast sitting next to Juicy, she kissed him on the cheek amicably.

"Daddy I'm glad you came to the club las' night," Juicy beamed earnestly.

"Oh really," Cool continued, "you jus' sayin' that, 'cause the dick was good," he bragged.

"It's not like that daddy, " Juicy uttered sincerely, "I enjoyed the dick, but you showed me a good time, an' that's somethin' I ain't had in awhile."

"I see, so what you think your beau gon' have to say 'bout that?" Cool asked on the sly.

"I ain't worried, so you shouldn't be either."

"Dig that," Cool continued. "I'ma be straight up wit'cha...first gimme a hint to what I was gettin' at las' night."

Jus' 'cause I dance, don't mean I'ma dupe. I can read between the lines well kinfolk," Juicy replied mockingly, as they both chuckled. "I used to have a pimp..." She was cut off.

"Say no mo' baby girl," Cool intervened, "I jus' like to run it down without sounding too harsh, know-wha'-I'm-talkin'-'bout?"

Juicy chuckled girlishly. "Daddy you didn't offend me," she continued, "I need a backbone,'cause the niggah I'm wit' now don't know what he want."

"Dig that. So it's settled then," Cool assured, "all I have to do is continue settin' up shop... I'll take it that I can depend on you, right?"

"No doubt, come by the club later I'ma surprise you" Juicy assured; kissing him tenderly on the cheek. "But there's one mo' thing I mus' tell you though," she sighed.

Cool's smile turned into a frown of curiosity. Hopefully there were no deterrents that would stop him from obtaining a percentage of her dough, he thought.

"What is it baby girl?" Cool asked with suspicion.

"Well…" Juicy procrastinated. "I have a child."

"From Mr. Right I presume?" Cool quipped with a smirk.

"Cool!" Roxanne intervened from the other room. "Star wanna holla at you!"

Roxanne had no idea she was disrupting them. "Tell her she gon' have to hol' on, I'm talkin' shop!" Cool roared. He wasn't rushing to the phone, since she stood him up last night. "Now baby girl, before we were rudely interrupted," he continued impressively. Juicy displayed a smile; elated that he didn't run to the phone like a wimp. "I wantcha to know I love kids, even though I don't have any of my own… I'm jus' here to alleviate the pains an' strengthen the gains. I wouldn't allow you to condemn your child, regardless of my tactics," he emphasized. "My management plus your dedicated hard work, equals success that will benefit us all, ya-feel-me?"

"Cool! She said if you don't come to the phone, she comin' up here!" Roxanne intervened again in the distance.

"Tell her to stop trippin', a niggah be there ina minute!" Cool shouted back, as he and Juicy chuckled. "Besides, we'll be long gone before she make it!"

"Daddy go see what she want. I understan' where ya comin' from, besides, you need all the hoes on the roster you can get, right?" Juicy announced with understanding.

He got up and strolled in the next room where Roxanne was still gossiping.

"Here he is girl, "Roxanne said through the receiver as he entered the room. "I see Juicy knew how to get your motor runnin', huh?" she commented.

"Perhaps that's correct," Cool sneered, "judgin'from the little performance earlier, I ain't the only engine she revved up," he snickered; while she handed him the receiver; simultaneously shooting him the middle finger. "Gone get ready baby girl, 'cause when I finish rappin' we gon' bounce," he ordered before he spoke through the receiver. "Why you rushin' a niggah to the phone man, when you showed ya ass las' night, huh?" he responded with a stern tone.

Star recognized his irateness, realizing she disrespected the game, but has plans to make up for her blunder. "Baby I'm sorry, "she began apologetically. "I was chasin' somethin' that continues to run away," she sighed sincerely.

"Well, be that as it may," Cool disregarded, "I jus' wanted you to know you ain't slick as cat shit, know-wha'-I'm-talkin'-'bout? She burst out in laughter, but he didn't. He wanted her to feel the intensity within him; knowing in order to dominate women he had to be indignant, as well as caring. "I ain't trippin', I see you think I'm some type of toy or some shit!" he roared; distracting her laughter.

"Don't be like that baby, I was jus' trippin off what you jus' said." Star informed earnestly. "But if you don't wanna be bothered, cool by me Mr. Cool."

"It's like this baby girl, I don't like bein' stood up, feel me?"

"I tell ya what baby boy, I don't have to work today, let's discuss an' get more aquainted over dinner," Star suggested.

"I can't promise dinner, due to my hectic schedule. However, we can fall in Chili's or somthin' later tonight," Cool assured; not wanting to cancel his date with Angel and Lil Red.

"Sounds good to me," Star replied.

As he strolled back into the adjoining room, he noticed the broads still nibbling on their breakfast fruit.

"Well kids, it' been fun, but a niggah gotta run!" Cool announced.

"We ready daddy," Juicy said; springing from the sofa, while Roxanne followed suit.

Once they made it down to the lobby, the ofay patrons gawked at him contemptuously. Probably, because he had two scantily clad beauties strutting on each side of him, he thought. As they walked up to the counter to check out, the ofays displayed a warm smile, but he knew what that meant. Therefore, he returned the fuck you smile back at them. After he checked out, Cool tipped the valet then sped off.

Betrayal of Peers

Chapter – 12

Whiile driving down the 610 Freeway on his way to his mom's house to meet D.J., Cool's mentality methodically transitioned from mack mode to dope dealer. Since he was running a tad bit late, he decided to call his mom to make sure his guest was there waiting.

"Hey momma," Cool began, "my homeboy there waitin' for me?"

"Ain't nobody came by," Ms. Hudson replied.

"Do me a favor baby girl, an' see if somebody sittin' in the driveway."

" Hol' on for a minute," Ms. Hudson replied; placing the phone down. She walked to the window and peeped out, noticing there was a strange vehicle parked in her driveway. Unfazed, because it was someone for her son, she welcomed his guest inside with hospitality. "Y'all get out an' come inside!" she insisted; grasping their attention, as she bellowed out the door. They displayed cordial smiles, as they were getting out the car. "Y'all could've knocked on the door."

"We jus' decided to wait on Coo... I mean Carlos in the driveway ma'am. So how ya doin'?" D.J. asked.

"I'm fine," Ms. Hudson replied.

"My name D.J. this Spencer," he introduced himself.

"How ya doin' ma'am," Spencer greeted magnanimously.

"I'm fine," Ms. Hudson reiterated, as they followed her inside the house. "You boys like somethin' to drink?"

"No thank you," They both replied in unison.

"Well, Carlos there on the phone, if y'all like to speak wit' him," Ms. Hudson informed.

"Yes ma'am," D.J. spoke up, as he glanced at the phone on the table. "Is that the phone over there ma'am?"

"Yes, gon' pick it up, I guess he still on there," Ms. Hudson indicated.

Cool awaited patiently for his mother to return to the phone, when a familiar voice spoke instead. "I'm 'bout fi'teen minutes from ya dawg, my bad it's takin' me so long, but I had to drop them boppas off firs', know-wha'-I'm-talkin'-'bout?"

Approaching the house, Cool smiled at his homie sitting in the car with some other cat. He noticed a massive cloud of smoke escaping their ride, when his comrade and associate stepped out the car to greet him.

"What's up kinfolk?" D.J greeted, as he took a hit of the blunt.

"What's goin' down?" Cool chuckled as they entered his ride.

"This here my niggah Spencer," D.J. introduced.

"Wha'd up kinfolk? This niggah dragged you way down here, huh?" Cool joked.

"Yeah," Spencer chuckled, giving him dap from the back seat.

"I ain't have no otha choice," D.J. added, "my slab down an' this niggah, the only niggah I trus' to bring me, ya dig?" he emphasized; taking a hit of the blunt, before trying to pass it to Cool.

"Thanks, but no thanks," Cool reneged, "I ain't tryna get no dirty piss this early in the game."

"I feel ya dawg, a niggah like me be on that Zydot, ya dig? I gotta have my trees... So Cool, what's ya proposition?" he switched topics.

"Tell ya what," Cool paused, "I believe in you so, I'ma slide you half a brick. However, I need to see you in a few days. Think ya can handle that?"

D.J. displayed a jovial expression. There was no way he was letting this opportunity slip through his fingertips, he thought. Even though his comrade Spencer was laid back smoking the blunt, D.J. knew he was also observing their discussion. He didn't mind Spencer knowing about the dope, but knowing about the price was an entirely different matter. Therefore, he kindly commanded Spencer to step. Giving him the task to roll another blunt, while he continued conversing with Cool.

"Damn right I can handle that," D.J. replied.

Cool gave him a decent price he could prosper from. It was just fifty dollars higher than what he planned to let ounces go for in Houston. He did this to facilitate the three day deadline, and make the fish bite harder, so to speak.

"Soun' like a plan to me," D.J. beamed. "So when do we get this show on the road?"

"As soon as I go to the lab an' bake it. I won't be long."

"Ah'ight dawg, waitin' on you then," D.J. assured.

CS

Black was still laying in bed, when his phone woke him up out of his slumber.

"Hello," Black grumbled wearily; still drained from the previous night's sexcapade.

"Rise an' shine, it's pimpin' time!" Cool began with zeal. "Did yo' wife beat that ass for comin' in so late?!" he pestered comically.

"What the fuck you want?" Black growled. "Do you ever sleep niggah?"

"Don't nothin' come to a sleeper but a dream kinfolk," Cool chuckled, "I need ya assistance dawg," he said switching topics.

"Shhh…. It's gon' have to be later on I'm tired," Black fumed; breathing heavy in a low tone.

"Naw niggah, it can't wait. I'll be through ina jif'," Cool said persuasively.

"Man if you come by my crib, I'ma shoot cha dead in the ass for disturbin' me," Black uttered placidly, as they both chuckled at his sarcasm. "An' when five-o ask what happen, I'ma tell him I caught you climbin' out my window."

They continued roaring with laughter.

"Come on kinfolk, it's beneficial for both of us, besides, you wouldn't shoot your number one bread winner," Cool responded relentlessly with a chuckle.

"You jus' ain't gon' let a niggah get no rest is ya?" Black responded with a sigh. "When you wanna stop by?"

"Within the next twenty minutes, Cool replied.

"Ah'ight damn fool… Later," Black signed off.

Since Cool took a shower back at the hotel, he put on some smell good and another dapper new outfit, before prepping painstakingly in the mirror. On his way out the door, he waved goodbye; as his nose detected the scrumptious cuisine his mother was preparing. She offered to feed his face again, but he opted not to, since he was on a quest for financial enhancement. He vowed to come back for a plate later, knowing she has skills like a gourmet chef.

CS

Still puffing on a blunt, sitting in Cool's mom's driveway, D.J. and Spencer displayed egregious looks toward each other, when the abrupt approach of a strange vehicle pulled up. Cool chuckled within, as he sat behind the tinted up vehicle imagining how startled they were. Since he never paged them, they had no idea he changed from luxury to incognito. Once Cool let down the window, their angst emotions faded away when they got a visual on who he was. D.J hopped out the car and scampered in his direction, grinning.

"Damn niggah!" D.J. gibbered upon his approach. "Yo' ass full of surprises, we didn't know who the fuck you was!"

"I figured that," Cool chuckled. "Gon' get back in ya ride, I'll be over there ina minute," he uttered evasively; rudely rolling up his window.

"Ah'ight playa," D.J. replied, as he strolled away submissively.

Impervious of how his associate felt, Cool deemed it too early in the game to divulge the secret compartments. D.J. was being put on a probation he knew nothing about.

After stashing the crack inconspicuously under his shirt, Cool slammed the lid back on the spot, and hopped in the other car manifesting the unlawful goodies.

"Ah'ight kinfolk, here ya go," Cool continued concisely. "This eighteen, y'all be careful on the highway." He gave them both dap and got out strolling toward his car.

D.J. bellowed out to him.

"Look out Cool!" D.J hollered

"Wha'd up though?!" Cool replied; turning around on his heels.

"Ya know where a niggah can cop some lean?" D.J. asked.

"Shh... not really, but my kinfolk might," Cool transitioned cautiously. "Y'all already ridin' dirty enough dawg. You don't need to be bullshttin' on the highway, know-wha'-I'm'-talkin'-'bout?"

"You sure right my niggah. I ain't finna let nothin' happen to the work, if so, I'll cover it, ya dig?"

"I hope so my niggah," Cool chuckled seriously; pondering how in the hell his destitute homie would be able to cover it, especially since he was just getting started.

"It's drought season on that shit down my way."

"I feel ya fool, let me give my cousin a call, I bet he know where to get it... Hell, he might even be sellin' it," Cool gloated.

When Cool gave Lou a call, he was laying on his ass – as usual at that time of day – but had what they were looking for, indeed.

"Hol' on Lou," Cool said through the receiver, as he got D.J.'s attention. "How much of this shit you want?!" he shouted.

"I ain't got much scrilla on me! Tell him a eight or somethin'!" D.J. shouted back; standing by the car conversing with Spencer.

"Don't sweat it homie my treat!" Cool entertained.

"Good lookin' out!" D.J. replied thankfully.

"Look out Lou," Cool began talking back into the receiver. "My homie want a eight, whatever that is," he uttered unaware… "Oh, it's eight ounces. How much that shit cost?" "That ain't bad, take it off the bill…" "Quit cryin' niggah, ya owe me…" "Ah'ight! I'ma tell him how to get there…" "Stop whinin' he straight, ya let them otha fake ass niggahs come by ya spot…" "Ah'ight." "Later." He hung up giving directions to his homie the best he could. Since Big Lou's house was near Timmy Chan's, D.J. apprehended quickly. "One mo' thang before ya bounce dawg, when you make it to the ponderosa, put a bunch of ones across my pager, so I know ya straight."

"Ah'ight playboy," D.J. acknowledged, "I should find ya kinfolk crib wit' no prob', an' when I finish this batch, I'ma get a celly so we can communicate better."

"No doubt," Cool replied, "be careful baby boy an' have a safe trip."

Waving at them as he sped off, Cool decided to head on over to Black's house to swap rides again. Glancing at the clock on the stereo, he decided to call Angel to see if they were ready. Which, she confirmed they would be by the time he arrived.

Betrayal of Peers

Chapter – 13

Finding Angel's house was a breeze since Cool was familiar with the area. Pulling inside the apartment building's parking lot, he noticed her car and parked abreast to it. The weather was humid as hell, he thought, as he strolled around in search of her apartment. Once he phoned her on his cell phone confirming the apartment number, she stepped out the door searching for him.

"Over here!" Angel shouted. He spotted her and walked toward her direction. "Come on in we almost ready."

Cool sighed. "It's hotter than a Mexican plate lunch out there! This A/C feel good!" he replied, as he flopped down on the sofa. Angel's mom and Lil' Red appeared once they heard the strange voice coming from the living room. "How ya doin' Ms. Wright?" he greeted cordially.

"I'm fine," Ms. Wright replied; strolling to the kitchen, then back to her bedroom.

As Ms. Wright disappeared, she informed her grandson to have fun.

"What's up Lil' Red?" Cool greeted; grasping her son's attention.

"What's up?" Lil' Red meekly replied.

"You remind me so much of ya daddy it's a shame," Cool continued; noticing the frown on Angel's mug at his opinion. "Where you want to go, it's your day little homie?"

"Ooh! Momma can we go to Toy's R Us?" Lil' Red asked gleefully.

"I tol' ya it was your day. You don't have to ask her, jus say the word," Cool reassured.

"You heard him Red. Don't ask me," Angel smirked, "it's his money we spendin' anyway," she responded, while heading out the door on their way to where a kid can be a kid.

Once they arrived at the toy store, Lil' Red got the bike of his choice, and a Nintendo Gameboy. Cool was elated to see the kid so jovial about his new gifts.

"I'm hungry, y'all wanna get somethin' to eat?" Cool announced; holding his stomach like he was starving.

"I am too," Lil' Red uttered.

"You like Mexican food little homie?" Cool asked; remembering a Spanish restaurant nearby.

"Yep," Lil Red assured.

"Good, 'cause I seen a Ninfas 'cross the street," Cool informed, as he continued. "What about you mama?"

He averted his attention toward Angel.

"I don't care where we eat," Angel responded.

"Well Mexican it is then, senor, senorita," Cool joked, as they headed off to appease their appetites.

Once they were seated at a table by the hostess, they ordered appetizers, a couple of tropical cocktails, and a soda for the kid.

As they continued to nibble on their appetizer, Lil' Red accidently spilled some soda, that cascaded off the table onto Cool's trousers. He jumped up from the table as if he sat on a tack. The agility of his movement brought tears of laughing hysteria to Angel and her son's eyes.

"Oh, so y'all think that shit funny, huh?" he seethed with anger, as he glanced down at the liquid permeating through his pant's leg. Good thing the soda was Sprite, he thought. "Ah'ight y'all wanna play ruff! Food fight!" he screamed, as the other patrons nearby gawked at his sudden alacrity.

Cool then grabbed two hands full of chips, crushed them, and threw them in both their faces, intentionally.

"Man!" Lil Red began. "It's on now!"

Lil Red began tossing chips back while his mom assisted him. They continued scampering about the table tossing chips back and forth, until their crunchy ammunition scattered everywhere.

"Damn we made a mess!" Angel chuckled, as she proceeded like a maid partially tidying up.

"Fagetaboutit," Cool began, "I'ma break the waitress off proper, let her do her job… Little homie you havin' fun?!"

"Yep!" Lil' Red smiled with a twinkle in his eye.

"That's good" Cool replied, as he was cut short by the vibration of his pager. "Damn who the hell could this be interrupting my fun!" he responded, as they chuckled at him.

Scanning his pager, Cool knew who the culprit was intervening in on the enjoyable time he was having. As he made the call, Angel and her son conversed in small talk; while eating their Mexican grub. Black didn't want nothing in particular, but to invite him to a social gathering at Jerry's house. They played the dirty dozen with each other for a little while. Thereafter, Cool agreed to stop by, as long as it was okay for his company to tag along.

CS

As Black crapped out for the fifth time, he shook his head in ridicule. Flustered by the loot he lost. The dice just weren't in his favor, he thought. The ringing of his cellular phone brought him out of his ill-fated reverie.

"Hello!" Black snapped; while the crowd laughed at his cantankerous demeanor. "Shit dawg, I'm gettin' my ass tore out the frame…" "Yuh that's the name of the street…" "You almost here fool, jus' keep comin on down…" "You'll see my slab parked on the curb…" "You see it?" "Ah'ight later," he hung up.

Once the car stopped, Lil' Red woke up as if he was programmed to do so. They all made their way toward the front door, rung the doorbell, and were greeted cordially by the lady of the house.

"Hi y'all doin'?" Jerry's wife greeted. "Come on in."

As they entered they all mutually introduced themselves.

Cool noticed all the fellas were upstairs. After he introduced himself, he headed in that direction; leaving the ladies, as well as Lil' Red be.

"Well Angel my name's Sharon, pleased to meet you," she diverted toward Lil' Red. "Lil' Red, the kids are out in the backyard, you can go out there an' play wit' 'em if ya like."

"Yes… I mean yes ma'am," Lil' Red replied properly; when his mother displayed a wanton look at him.

"You can gone on back there," Sharon chuckled, as she pointed in the direction. "He so cute," she continued; changing topics. "Girl do you know how to play poker?" she asked Angel.

"Yes, an' I hope y'all playin' for money," Angel replied insolently, as they both chuckled at her remark.

They entered the kitchen area where the other wives and girlfriends were. After they all mirthfully got acquainted with the newcomer, they dealt her a hand and continued playing.

Meanwhile, upstairs, boisterous laughter and shit talking brothers stood around a pool table with cash in their hands. Cool observed patiently; waiting on the right moment to partake in the lucrative crap game that was taking place. He also noticed Jim strolling around playing bartender; offering margaritas to everyone.

"What's up Cool, you want some of this?!" Jerry welcomed, as he rolled the dice across the table.

"Don't mind if I do kinfolk, jus' waitin' on my turn, know-wha'-I'm-talkin'-'bout?!" Cool informed, as he diverted his attention. "Jim baby, I'll have one of them if you don't mind!"

"Here ya go brotha," Jim granted; passing Cool one of the sweet intoxicants displayed on the tray.

"Cheer up Black," Cool teased; observing the distraught look on his homie's mug. I'ma rescue you boy," he emphasized, "I feel lucky t'day, jus' ride wit' me."

"I hope ya right baby boy," Black sighed.

"How much you lose fool?" Cool asked curiously.

"'Bout seventy-five hun'," Black flustered.

"Dizzam!" Cool grimaced.

"It's all good," Black chuckled, "I ain't trippin'… Look atcha boy Ray over there."

"I didn't even know that damn fool was wit'cha," Cool cackled. "Where he at?" He scanned the area in search of him.

"Over there by the T.V. on the couch," Black replied; pointing in his direction.

Cool walked in the vicinity to see Ray snoring; inebriated from one too many drinks. The sight was amusing as he erupted with laughter. His alacrity caused the crap game to cease, as everyone else gathered around Ray laughing, criticizing his drunken stupor.

Resuming the crap game, Cool noticed a few familiar faces, and was introduced to the ones he didn't know. Including a cat that is a police officer on Jerry's payroll.

It was now Cool's turn to shoot. He entered the crap game on fire; rolling seven and eleven out the door. Black took heed and rode with him, winning his loot back; plus four thousand interest.

Cool didn't gamble much, but when he did, he had the Midas touch, with the reward/risk ratio solely in his favor. He tore down the house fifteen thousand dollars richer – since they were shooting five hundred to a thousand a wop. The intensity and the noise caused some of the women to come upstairs to see what the commotion was all about.

Jerry was a chain gambler, but it wasn't his day. Obsessed with the sport, he didn't know when to quit. That's why he was the one to lose the most.

It wasn't a matter of paying the house initially, but Cool felt obligated; since he accumulated a nice wad. So, when the dice went cold, he raised up leaving the table victorious. Placing ten hundred dollar bills on the table, but still fifteen thousand dollars richer.

"It was nice doin' businesses wit' you boys," Cool boasted, "but I'ma take the money an' run."

Everyone was content, except Jerry, as they all congratulated him on his winnings.

Since Black was leaving also, Cool helped him carry Ray to the car. Black became irate at Ray's excessive drinking habits, since he constantly had to guide his alcoholic homie during his failed equilibrium stages.

"Ah'ight fool, ina minute," Cool chuckled, as they got in their cars and drove their separate ways.

CS

They arrived at the Hilton hotel near Angel's place thirty minutes later. Cool hopped out the car to go check in, leaving Angel and Lil' Red behind. He didn't plan to make any sexual passes at her, but the alcohol he imbibed earlier was gradually arousing his lustful nature. On the other hand, Angel sat in the car promiscuously pondering whether to let him take advantage of her. Her attraction for him was growing deeper by the minute.

Once he checked in, he strolled back to the car to get them. He figured they could just kick back for awhile, which was something she agreed to earlier. As they entered the room, he noticed it had two beds. Since Lil' Red was still in a state of slumber, he cautiously laid him down on one of the beds; trying not to wake him.

Suddenly, Cool's manly member garnered total control over of his righteous way of thinking, as he approached Angel French kissing her; at the same time guiding her on the other bed. This was something he never imagined, but when you're alone with a woman with a little liquor in your system, sex is bound to happen, he thought.

"What are we doin'?" Cool paused with guilty feelings.

"We kissin' baby," Angel purred; continuously kissing him tenderly on the lips; simultaneously unbuttoning her pants. "What's the matter?" she cooed.

"It jus'… Nothin'," he continued on; discarding the qualms he knew he would endure later on.

He stopped kissing and divested his gear; displaying his erect rod. Then, he patiently watched her squeeze out of the tight jeans she had on. Once they were in their birthday suits, they glanced over to see if the kid was still sleep – and he was.

Cool then lifted Angel's legs, placed them on his shoulder – with her willingness-and inserted his stiff dick in her pulsating pussy; pumping and pleasing until he exploded all his juices inside of her. He didn't bother using a condom since she was not a promiscuous person. But the thought of her getting pregnant never entered his mind, though.

"We not suppose to be doin' this," Cool regretted, as he rest his body on top of hers.

"Why not?" You actin' like we kin or somethin'," Angel purred; kissing him on the cheek; wanting him to take her again.

"Well, it's jus' th…" he began, as she cut him off.

"Look baby, I know how you feel," she consoled, "jus' 'cause I used to mess wit' cha cousin don't mean nothin', hell I told you we wasn't even together before he died," she expressed.

"I know, but it's jus' my way of thinkin' right now," he uttered elusively.

He wanted to keep his exploitation of her to a minimum and he did not want to hurt her feelings. She was the kind and considerate type that would make a good housewife. But since his ex-girlfriend Trina left him hanging, he wasn't looking to be tied down any time soon. It was a time to explore, pander, and get a little buck fucking wild! he thought.

"So... What's your way of thinkin'?" Angel asked curiously.

"I'ma keep it real wit'cha baby girl," Cool sighed, "I'ma playa. Ya know I jus' sever the ties of a previous relationship, or should I say, they severed me," he smirked concisely, "therefore, I..." She cut him short again.

"Baby I know ya hurtin' from your last relationship, I don't wanna interfere wit'cha plans... I jus' want to be wit' you... Ya know my momma tol' me that this would probably happen," she smirked.

"Oh, she did eh?" he leered.

"Yuh," she chuckled, "I didn't think I would feel this way so soon, though... I done fell in love, an' I want to be wit' you, I don't care about nothin' else," she mumble sincerely in his ear.

"Okay, you sayin' that shit now, but I'm tryna warn ya" he sighed, before she cut him short again; placing her finger over his lips; impervious of his bickering.

"It don't matter to me," she continued; licking around the aureole part of his nibbles. "I jus' wanna be wit' you," she moaned; attempting to get him back sexually aroused.

He giggled impishly, at the tickling touches of her tongue.

"Baby," she paused, "ya think if I help you get a house, I can move in wit'cha?"

He didn't plan on a consort, but having a woman and kid around would make the scenery appear more like home. Inconspicuous of drug trafficking, he thought. Even though he didn't want to get involved in another relationship so soon, he knew deep within he needed an intellectual woman that he could really trust on his team. Generally, she could assist him with his legitimate affairs; while he simultaneously appointed another steadfast female to help him oversee some of his illicit endeavors.

Pondering the details, as well as the platonic love he had for Angel and her son, helped make his spontaneous decision final. Which was to; have his cake and eat it too; as the saying goes.

"I tell ya what baby girl," Cool said, as he got out the bed; walking toward the lavatory to spruce up. "You can come along, but don't say I didn't warn ya," he chuckled; shaking his head. Angel followed behind slapping him on his bare ass. "Ouch!" he shrieked.

"Aw niggah, that didn't hurt," Angel teased; jovial from his decision. "Why ya not giving me no mo' pooh?" she cooed erotically; groping his bare butt cheeks. "Come on baby, I want some mo'" she moaned.

"Come on now baby girl, I tol' my peeps I was gon' hook up wit' him later… You can chill here if ya like, an' I'll give ya some mo' later," he offered courteously; hoping she opted not to stay, since he had other plans.

"I thought you wasn't workin' today?" She recollected.

"I'm not," he assured, "I jus' need to have a little powwow wit' my kinfolk, know-wha'-I'm-talkin'-'bout?"

He then turned the shower on and invited her to join him. As they bathe each other, they conversed about the future. She decided to go back home; since she had to go to work in the morning.

After they finished they got dressed, woke up the kid, and then headed to Angel's apartment.

Betrayal of Peers

Chapter - 14

Glancing at the clock radio, Cool decided to phone Star to see if she was still good to go on their date. He was also curious to know what she had to say about the mystery man in the Mercedes. He dialed her number vigorously, hoping the broad wasn't out of pocket. As he waited for her to answer, he reminisced about the fun he had earlier with his new found family, and the loot he beat for fair and square. The phone continued to ring until a drowsy voice finally answered.

"Hello," the voice murmured.

"Is Star there?" Cool asked.

"This she," Star indicated. "Who's this?"

"Damn baby girl, you sound like shit," Cool chuckled insolently. "This ya boy Cool, you forgot about our date, or what?"

"Naw niggah," she giggled, "you was takin too long, I went to sleep shit... Where ya at?"

"Ready to come scoop you, so get off ya ass," he jeered.

"You don't even know where I live niggah," she sneered, "let me give you directions."

She resided in the Southwest part of town. Once she gave him the verbal map, he found her residence with no problem. The apartments she lived in looked tranquil enough, he thought, as he followed another car through the security gate. Being wary is a sixth sense he developed from street life.

So, he remained vigilant of any perils that might be lurking in the night, as he strolled toward her unit.

Since there wasn't a doorbell, he knocked. The abrasive texture of the door caused him to rub his knuckles afterwards.

"Hey what's up?" Star answered. "Come in, I'm almost ready."

Her persona was very erotic. She flaunted a tight mini skirt, with a matching halter top blouse, revealing her smooth brown skin. And, judging the way her onion shaped ass swayed, she wasn't wearing panties either. He admired her appeal. He could tell she was a woman who enjoyed her profession, and these were the type of females he needed in his stable. Uninhibited hoochies who was down for flaunting the goods for a substantial amount of loot – whether dancing or fucking.

"Well, I'm ready!" she announced; taking him out of his reverie, as she appeared from the bedroom with some six inch heels on, to make her seductive outfit complete.

"Let's dip then baby girl," Cool began, as he rose up from the sofa. "I must say you look tasty," he licked his lips lasciviously, as he scanned her from head to toe.

"I'll take that as a complement, an' jus' might let cha eat me later," Star joked, as they both cackled at her arousing remark.

"Whaatevah," he smirked, "I bet you'll love that, huh?"

As they got in the car, he decided to take her to Chili's restaurant and bar. Something with a nice atmosphere; but not too extravagant.

Cruising along she unzipped his pants. Her tender touch stimulated his flaccid member. He relaxed, stayed focused on the road, and relished the sensational dick massage she laid on him. Until he regained his senses; realizing he hadn't totally confronted her about the cat in the Mercedes. He wanted to see if the mystery man would pose a threat to what he was after.

"Oh yeah, niggah," Cool sneered; causing her to pause. "I know you don't owe me no explanation, but that shit you pulled the otha night botherin' me. I'm not jealous, but when I'm after somethin', I don't need shit standin' in my way." He put his dick back in his pants; feigning like he was upset.

"You still on that?" she grimaced. "You ain't gotta worry about him."

"Ah'ight," he continued. "So, what the niggah mean to you, then?"

"He's jus' my ex, we don't fuck around no mo'," she expressed with an evasive look on her mug.

"Yuh, right!" he shot back; noticing her posture. "My instinct tellin' me the flame still lit."

"Boy please," she sneered, "I'd be lyin' if I said I didn't have love for him, but I'm not in love wit' him no mo'."

They finally made it to their destination; noticing the place wasn't crowded, as they got out the car. "I jus' hope I'm not gettin' myself caught up in no fatal attraction shit"

"Boy please. Let's go inside," Star replied.

"Lookout," Cool snarled, "I heard that boy shit twice, watch your mouth, now."

"Niggah" Star chuckled at his defensiveness. "It's jus' a figure of speech... Okay! What do you prefer daddy?"

"All the while," he retorted, "soun' mo' noble to me."

"Yuh, right."

The hostess then cordially greeted; making a futile attempt to show them to a table. But they declined; preferring to sit at the bar. Star ordered a gin and juice from the bartender, while Cool ordered a Remy Martin on the rocks, and two helpings of Buffalo wings.

"Baby girl sit tight, I'll be right back, I left my phone in the ride," Cool indicated.

"Ah'ight daddy," Star replied compliantly.

Once Cool made it back, they ate the rest of the wings and imbibed liquor for a couple of hours. Cool noticed the cocktails were having an effect on Star's demeanor.

She outwardly fondled his dick through the exterior of his pants. And he allowed her to carry on.

"You like that daddy," Star cooed; licking her lips seductively.

"Already," Cool replied complacently. His inner psyche told him that the timing was perfect to elaborate on the subject of pandering. "I'm not tryna disturb your groove babygirl." he emphasized. "But do you recall what I was talkin' 'bout at the club when we firs' met?"

"I forgot daddy," she murmured; continuing her lewd ritual. "Refresh my memory."

"Well... Part of my charm from the otha night have a lot to do wit' me wantin' to delve in the panderin' business," he revealed concisely.

"Ya know it's funny you mention that, it's a lot of hoes lookin' for management," she continued, as he listened attentively; admiring her candid character. "I used to give my ex all my cho-chos. I'm quite familiar wit' the game. But I have to love you though, an' the feelings gotta be mutual."

"Right on," he nodded in agreement. "If I said I love you right now, I'd be lyin' through my teeth." They both chuckled, as he continued. "However, there is adulation at this point, know-wha'-I'm-talkin'-'bout? You don't appear to me as havin' any strings attach... Then, again, do you have any kids?" he asked curiously.

"Hell naw!" she denounced with emphasis. "Don't get me wrong, I love'em, now, but I'm not tryna have none no time soon... Okay?!"

"Dig that," he continued. "So why you an' dude split up?"

"That niggah forgot who helped him get on his feet... Hell, I bought that Benz he drive," she said presumptuously.

"So, you like that, huh?" he smirked; boosting her ego.

"Let's jus' say, I get mine... Okay?!" she bragged.

"So, baby girl," he switched to serious mode, "if you down wit' the program, an' you should see me fraternizin' wit' another female, I take it you wouldn't trip, because it comes with the territory."

"I'm not jealous daddy, but I have a pet peeve... I gotta be the main one. "So do you have a woman?"

"Not exactly," he lingered, as he continued, "it's this girl I care about, but that situation has nothin' to do wit' the electrifyin' world I plan to develop wit' you," he promised.

"Em-hm. So you already have a girlfrien'," she assumed skeptically.

"Call it whatcha want, but it won't interfere in what we have. Besides, she's jus' as beneficial as you can possibly be on the real."

Star took a swig of her drink, displaying a wanton look on her mug. Cool could tell she was taking the bait. Maybe she was trying to make her ex-man jealous, or perhaps she was just lonely and needed a backbone, he thought. Whatever it was, she suddenly became submissive to his deeds, and kissed him on the lips before she continued.

"I usually don't give in so soon, but I mus' say I was attracted to you from the start. I'm not worried 'bout your girlfrien'. She'll be the queen of her domain, an' I'll be the queen of mine... Okay? I kno a few girls that will be down too," she assured dutifully.

He displayed a sly grin at her decision, while maintaining his composure.

"I'm thrilled, you'll be my lieutenant, so to speak... So, what's the deal wit' Juicy?" he asked.

"Whataya mean?" she replied.

"She act like she down."

"My, we move fast don't we," she replied comically.

"Well, ain't no need in waitin', that shit broke the wagon a long time ago, know-wha'-I'm-talkin'-'bout?" They both chuckled. "Besides, a niggah gotta accrue mo' females, huh?"

"True," she agreed, "Juicy ah'ight... I mean. Oh, I know. Did she tell you she got a baby daddy? Not boyfrien' now. BABY DADDY!!!!!!!" she emphasized.

"Baby girl, yous a damn fool!" he smirked.

"If she wanna get down for her crown, I ain't mad at her. But, I seen that niggah beat her ass in Foxes before," she assured.

"Hmm," he gruffed, "she didn't mention that"

"Well, he dragged her ass outta Foxes one night, I know that much."

"So, o' girl got issues. Perhaps I can be a scapegoat of some sort. It's about mind over matter, not how much blood you splatter."

"Well, everybody ain't as smooth as you daddy," she lauded, as they both chuckled.

"I don't need no drama," he assured, as he continued," "but if her solidarity is as valid as she claim, she deserve to be rescued, ya-feel-me?"

"Well, all you can do is see daddy," she consoled; rubbing his leg gently.

"Already," he replied optimistically. "She wanted me to stop by the club tonight... She say she have a surprise for me."

"Let's go then daddy. We still got time," she implied.

"Ah'ight baby girl," he grinned.

While he drove pondering, Star laid snuggled under him from the time they left the restaurant. As she leered up at him, she noticed him in meditation.

"Penny for ya thoughts," Star uttered curiously.

"Well, I was jus' thinkin' 'bout when I was incarcerated. I used to envision one day of becomin' a proprietor of my own bordello of beautiful women. Women of various ethnicities, like my idol Larry Flynt, the dude who own the Hustler Corporation," he professed.

"Yeah, I know who you talkin'-'bout," she informed.

"Well," I notice how he went from illicit to legit, an' I basically have the same concept."

"Damn," she uttered. "I'm down wit'cha daddy."

"Tomorrow baby girl, I wantcha to look for a crib... I have a hunch matters will piece together," he said positively.

"Do you have a particular area in mind?"

"The southwest, ya know. Somewhere that looks respectable," he advised.

"I know somebody that can hook us up, I'll holla at him tomorrow, an' if we find somthin' I'ma call you," she informed.

"So, now all ya have to do is get ya ass in gear, an' shake your money maker," he hinted, as they both chuckled.

"I ain't trippin daddy I know I gotta bring somethin' to the table," she replied reliably; articulating his innuendo. Finally making it to Foxes, they noticed it wasn't crowded. "Befor we go inside daddy, I wantcha to know somethin'," she uttered; gasping his attention as they parked. "I prefer dancin' over anything else."

"Shit, I ain't got no problem wit' that," he smirked, "a trick is a trick... Trickin' his ass outta his evil faces is all that matter."

Star cackled admiring Cool's logical leniency.

"Don't get me wrong, now, if them trick ass niggahs cho-chos right, they can get some of this pussy. I ain't fuckin' for pennies.

"I feel ya baby girl," he grinned, "do whatcha deem necessary. As long as you meet the quota. Some might not perform as well as others," he uttered.

Cool wanted feedback on how much capital he should expect without sounding so demanding. Star read between the lines, took the bait, and replied back earnestly.

"Daddy at least three-four thousand a week, each girl. Now the less fortunate ones, nothin' less than two thousand," Star speculated from previous experiences.

"Hmm," Cool mumbled, "that will do for now."

"Whatcha say daddy?" she shot back inquisitively.

"Nothin'… Go in there an' get us a table, I gotta make a call, I'll be there ina minute. " he warded off.

"Okay daddy," she replied compliantly, before giving him a kiss, and proceeding on her way to oblige his command.

Being canny, Cool phoned Big Lou and invited him to the final hours of fun – as well as to watch his back from the unexpected. Willingly, his cousin accepted. He thought it ironic, how modern day pandering was so much different from old school pimping techniques. Back in the day, if a broad would have said she wasn't selling her pussy unless… Was like taking a chance on getting her ass beat.

Betrayal of Peers

Chapter - 15

As Cool entered the club with his genteel style, he could sense the stares from scoundrels of both genders. Gawking like wild animals anticipating the right moment to capture and devour helpless prey, he thought. Impervious, he strolled through highlighting the surroundings with his presence.

Then along came Carol, greeting him as if she had been expecting him. "Hey baby," she began, "Star tol' me you were outside. Follow me, I'll lead ya to your girls," she giggled knowingly.

"What's up baby girl? Ya been workin' hard?" Cool teased.

"Hell naw, baby!" Carol stressed. "But, I'm tryna get paid though!" They both chuckled, as she latched hold of his arm like an escort. "Baby, ya lookin good everytime I see you." she concluded courteously.

"Thankya baby girl," Cool expressed gratefully, as he continued. "Its essential for a cat of my caliber to represent to the fullest, ya dig?"

"I can dig it baby," Carol snickered. "Be back with ya'll drinks."

Cool noticed the mirth expressions of his female seducers. Judging from the jovial way they mingled, made him realize his dazzling stratagem had worked. He kissed them both, as he sat between the two of them in the booth.

"Hey daddy," Juicy enthused, "I got somethin' for you!"

"Dig that," Cool smirked. "Mus' be my surprise, huh?"

"I guess ya can call it that, know-wha-I'm-talkin'-'bout?" Juicy mocked jokingly; causing them to laugh. She then browsed inside a small purse mounted on her person, and handed him the seven hundred dollar bills it stored. "I kept fifty dollars of it daddy for gas, an otha miscellaneous," she confessed earnestly.

"Hm. I'll admit, I'm impress," Cool grinned convincingly; switching topics. "So... I noticed you ladies were conversin' befor I creeped up."

"If you mean a discussion, yes," Star frowned, as they all laughed. "Anyway, I was explainin' to her what need to be done daddy, an' how we plan to do it."

"An' I'm still down daddy," Juicy concurred. "Besides, I'm overdue for a change. That niggah gettin' on my nerves, shit!" she jolted seriously.

They chuckled at her slight tantrum.

"Consider that shit done baby girl," Cool assured. "Well..." he was cut short by the barmaid's sudden appearance.

"I'm back!" Carol announced, as she place their drinks on the table. "That didn't take long, did it?"

"Naw baby girl," Cool smiled, "go get ya-self a drink too."

"Thanks baby, don't mine if I do," Carol replied pleased.

Before Carol left, the light bulb of ideas went off in Cool's head. She was fairly attractive; compared to the hideous looking broads that held the same position. Plus her voluptuous rump shaker was something he knew his cousin would love.

"Look out Carol!" Cool hollered out; getting her attention before she disappeared.

"You need somethin' else baby?" Carol back tracked.

"Not yet baby girl, but I was wonderin' what cha got up after work. I jus' might have a proposition for ya," Cool indicated cunningly.

"Oh really," Carol smirked with sparkling eyes; while they all observed with glee.

"Yeah baby girl, my niggah will be here any minute, I wantcha to meet him," Cool replied amusingly.

"Well," Carol strained, "I'm grown, single…no curfew! My little boy over my mom's place, so if ya homie straight, we can arrange a date," she gestured, as they all chuckled.

"If he rollin' wit' me, he straight, besides, he's my cousin," Cool replied arrogantly.

"Okay baby, I ain't trippin'. Let me go get a drink, I'll be right back," Carol assured, as she attempted to stroll off.

"Befor ya bounce baby girl," Cool continued; grasping her attention again. "Be on the lookout for a heavy set fly ass niggah."

"Hmmm, heavy set, eh?" Carol smiled. "I like 'em chunky!" They all laughed at her honesty. "I'll be back!" she said wiggling her ass away.

"Now, baby girls," Cool diverted his attention back to his girls. "Where were we?"

Star began. "As I was sayin', I was fillin Juicy in on everything. I tol' her I was gonna be in charge of business affairs, an' I have a couple mo' hoes in mind who'll be down too."

"Tell y'all what," Cool added, "once we get settled, we'll recruit som' mo'. For now, y'all two will do, an' perhaps one mo'," he implied feasibly.

"I know Porsche ass will be down," Star blurted.

"Yuh, that bitch wild," Juicy included, "but I like her, she straight."

"Let's toas' then," Cool announced, as they all held up their glasses. "To a prosperous future, an' may all our dreams come true, 'cause if I get a stable as beautiful as y'all, ain't gon' be no stoppin' us," he carried on like a braggart to instill confidence in them both. "One mo' thang ladies, befor I forget."

"Yes daddy," they both replied in unison.

"I want us all to look at this as a business venture, an' y'all will be my constituents of leisure," Cool began, as the girls chuckled at his business oriented tactic. "We strivin' for professionalism, that pimp whore phrase is a little harsh nowadays."

The broads nodded their heads tacitly to his cleverness. Even though their clients were just tricks, they knew if tricks detected signs of being played too hard, it would shatter their images. Furthermore, running them off.

Closing time was near, and there still were no signs of Big Lou showing up. While sipping on their drinks, they all agreed on getting sexually busy after the club. This was another moment Cool longed for. The broads continued on gibbering about the future, while he pondered the ménage a trois that was about to go down, once they got to his hotel room.

Carol's sudden approach – along with Big Lou and some other slim framed, fearless looking cat – robbed Cool of his fantasy.

"Is this who you was talkin'-'bout baby?!" Carol beamed. "He's cute, a little shy at firs'though." she said teasingly.

"Ain't nothin' shy 'bout that niggah!" Cool replied jokingly, as they all laughed – with the exception of the stranger.

"Cooly, ya know I'm bashful... I ain't afraid of no pussy, though," Big Lou bantered; causing them all to break out in a laughing hysteria – once again, with the exception of the stranger.

"Bet not be. Ya know faggots ain't allowed within the family tree," Cool stressed. "Carol! Get my peeps whatever they want to drink! Y'all boys damn near didn't make it!" he continued on, as Carol took all their drink orders; then headed off to handle her duties.

By the time they all introduced each other, Carol showed back up with the drinks, and to get more acquainted with Big Lou. The outcome boiled down to a rendezvous back at Cool's hotel suite. During the hoopla, Cool observed how nonchalant and eerie Big Lou's estrange comrade was. The weirdo even used the name Ouija for a moniker. Everyone was in chill mode; except him. Judging by the vigilant way Ouija constantly case the joint.

Admiring Ouija's stalwart manner, gave Cool a gut feeling the new companion would become a useful factor of some sort. Attempting to alleviate the stranger's uneasiness, Cool beckoned for Juicy to perform a lap dance for him.

"Baby boy, relax, an' let my girl take ya mind off things," Cool accommodated; noticing Ouija was still unmoved.

"I don't wantcha to think I don't 'preciate nothin' man… I dig ya hospitality an' all, it's jus' me bein' me, doin' what I'm paid to do, know-wha'-I'm-talkin'-'bout?" Ouija replied patriotically.

His gesture amused the crowd, but his atrocious demeanor wouldn't allow his face to crack a smile.

"The club 'bout to close y'all!" Juicy announced, as she finished dancing. "Let me go get dress'd an' tip out!"

She hopped off of Ouija's lap to go end her night's worth of labor. Leaving her victim in awe, as he stared at the half clad thoroughbred sashay away.

"Well, let me go finish up too!" Carol included, "I'll be back big daddy!" she winked at Big Lou before she got off his lap.

"I'll be waitin' baby!" Big Lou replied with glee, as everyone chuckled.

The disc jockey announced last call for alcohol, while playing the last song for the night. They all could tell by the look in Star's eyes that she was intoxicated. She inserted her tongue in and out of Cool's ear; simultaneously whisper how she couldn't wait to freak him down. Cool could tell his counterparts accredited his wielding way with women.

Finally the moment of anticipation, Cool thought, as they all strolled out the club to get their freak on.

Just as they were getting inside their cars preparing to leave, some rotund six foot tall cat emerged out of nowhere approaching Juicy, as she was putting her dancing gear in the trunk of her car. Everyone sat in their cars observing the stranger's belligerent attitude while conversing with her.

"That's her baby daddy," Star declared; with her eyes glued to the drama.

"I can tell," Cool replied, "I guess this is the moment of truth," he sneered as he got out. He vowed to himself not to let her baby daddy abuse her in front of him – especially since he was now the chosen one. The homies scrutinized the drama also, awaiting for their cue to annihilate. As he approached the scene, he concentrated on his defensive; as well as offensive tactics. Over the years, he learned when coming into the perils of a fracas, one must be prepared. "Juicy baby ya ah'ight?!" he intervened.

"Yuh daddy, ain't nothin' I can't handle."

Her baby daddy made a futile slap attempt. Cool caught his useless swing with a follow up left cross; swiftly to his nose.

"Niggah ya need to learn how to be mo' courteous! Ya fuckin' woman beater!" Cool responded cantankerously; stepping back awaiting retaliation.

The blow stunned the now bloody nose abuser, but he wasn't a coward, as he commenced to defend his manhood.

"Mu'fucka! You should mine ya own biz!" her baby daddy sputtered, as he charged Cool like a wrestler.

"Juicy is my b'ness! Playa!" Cool gruffed, as he moved with agility; spinning out of his adversary's huge mitts.

It only took a minute before Ouija intervened in the scuffle. He came out of nowhere with a 9 mm Beretta in hand; pistol whipping Juicy's baby daddy upside the head until he hit the deck; blood oozing out rapidly from his skull. Juicy stood there screaming with terror, when Ouija climbed on top of her baby daddy's torso, and insatiably pound his head some more with the pistol. Damn near beating him unconscious.

"Don't kill him kinfolk! We don't need no murder rap!" Cool shouted remorsefully.

The gory scene dispelled the intrusive crowd that once looked on. One could hear the screeching of the spectators' tires, as they fled before they had to witness a murder.

"Ya oughta let me do this niggah, C baby!" Ouija seethed; pausing the brutal torture he put on the enemy.

"Now ain't the time dawg! Too many eyes, know-wha'-I'm-talkin'-'bout?!" Cool cautioned, as he continued. "Lou! Come get this damn fool!" he beckoned.

Big Lou was busy scrutinizing the cat who sat in the car that brought Juicy's baby daddy to the club. He had his 357 magnum, in hand, just in case the driver wanted to assist in the skirmish. Judging the cowardly look in the driver's eyes, he didn't want no trouble.

"Ouija!" Big Lou subdued. "Raise up, let the niggah make it! For now, at least," he mumbled. "A matter of fact we all need to raise up befor five-o come through!"

"Dig that!" Cool bellowed in agreement, as he frantically diverted his attention toward Juicy. "Baby girl, get in the car wit' Star, I'ma let this damn fool drive your car!" he said referring to Ouija. She scurried over to the cars startled from the gobs of blood she noticed protruding from her baby daddy's skull. "Oujia follow behind us in her car!" he continued.

"Ah'ight C baby!" Ouija replied; stepping away from his victim. "Jus' let me wipe some of this punk's blood off my hands! Bitch made mu'fucka might have AIDS!" he continued on; mean mugging his victim. "I think ya still should let me do him, though!" he sneered.

The victim whimpered like a wounded animal begging for his life; until Cool stood over him and assured his now disabled ass, not to fear; unless he tried to be Billy bad ass again.

"Gon' get in the car, let's dip. I think our friend got the message." Cool grinned diabolically toward Ouija, as he strolled toward his car.

Ouija did what he was commanded to do, while Big Lou approached the car of the victim's companion; with his gun in clear view. Initially, the cat was nervous, until Big Lou allayed his conscience.

"Look out homie," Big Lou began; tapping on his window. "Gon' getcha boy on outta here, the party over. We don't have no beef, but he did, so he had to pay for it, know-wha'-I'm-talkin'-'bout?"

"I... I... I understan'," the driver stuttered, as he rolled down his window. "He shouldn't have tried to whip on that girl any how... I tol' that niggah 'bout that shit," he dreadfully explained.

The driver then got out the car to help his incapacitated comrade. He empathized with his homie, as he observed him laying in a pool of blood. He also imagined how excruciating the pain was. There would be a few permanent stigmas upside the head, but at least he will live, the driver thought.

As they all rode in silence; crammed in the front seat, Cool noticed Star had her arm around Juicy consolingly. He started having guilty feelings about what Ouija did, but knew deep down inside, Juicy's baby daddy deserved a beat down for trying to get physical with her.

"Don't worry baby," Star relieved; breaking the silence, "he got what he had comin' to him."

Cool glanced over noticing tears cascading down Juicy's cheeks, and assisted in the comforting.

"Look out baby girl," Cool began, "I wasn't gon' let that niggah kick ya ass in front of me. I didn't think my homie was gon' react the way he did, but that's what he get paid for... like he said earlier," he assured seriously.

"Yuh daddy, I'm hip," Juicy uttered in a low soft tone. "But I thought Ouija was gon' kill him... I don't wish death on nobody," she stressed.

"I jus' raised baby girl," Cool stressed. "Ya think I wanna go back already? Or ever for that matter?! Ya said ya wanted a change of scenery... Well, ya locked in now!" he quipped. They all chuckled at his remarks. "Don't worry, baby girl,I gotcha, an' I got a soft spot in my heart for that bu'shit baby daddy of yours. I ain't got no mo' beef, but if he get out of line again, I wouldn't hesitate to turn my minions loose."

CS

"That little niggah crazy! I thought he was gon' kill Tank ass!" Carol distress to Big Lou, as they followed Cool into the parking lot of their destination.

Big Lou took a swig from the white Styrofoam cup – which was filled with codeine cough syrup and soda. The ghetto elixir that was becoming more popular than ever before, on the underground market. He passed the cup over to her, then grabbed the fry sticks that were in the ashtray; embedded in foil paper. As he lit the phencyclidine marijuana joint – he constantly kept an appetite for – he took two long hard pulls, until he felt the psychedelic affect. Then, he passed it to Carol before he replied to her remark.

"Ya kno Carol, we wouldn't let my niggah murdah nobody, we ain't no killahs, know-wha'-I'm talkin'-'bout?" he fabricated.

Carol listened attentively; taking a couple of drags off the green wet joint; nodding her head in agreement. "Here ya go baby," she harrumphed, passing him back both mind altering substances. "You gon' have me fuck'd up," she giggled.

"I be back kinfolk!" Cool bellowed back. "Lemme see if I can cop anotha suite next to mine!" he informed, before proceeding toward the entrance.

"Ah'ight kinfolk!" Big Lou replied.

"Big-baby," Ouija responded; rolling down the window, as he pulled along side of Big Lou. "Ya think Cool will let me borrow the wheels for a minute?"

"Hell naw niggah!" Big Lou sneered. "Where ya tryna go anyway?"

"This ain't my cup of tea kinfolk. I'ma go to the Alamo where I can feel at home….Besides, I'm geeking"

"If kinfolk letcha use his girl's ride, take ya ass straight to the Alamo, an' tell Jeff I said give you an eight-ball. That oughta hol' ya for awhile."

Even though they were both amused by his threat, Ouija never crossed Big Lou, and maintained his reverence as a loyal soldier. Although, Ouija didn't care much for partaking in sexual pleasures, his appetite for killin and destruction, is skills needed within the faction. Big Lou met him when they were both doing county jail bids, and been comrades every since.

Mostly because, Big Lou took care of him on the inside, providing necessities – just as he did now. Ironically, Ouija used to be an ordain minister, until the crack robbed him of his steadfast desire to preach the word. But being a dope fiend didn't deter his big heart; which made him one of the most feared cats, throughout the southside streets of Houston.

Cool finally approached with some good news. He was fortunate enough to get an adjoining room.
Inconspicuously, Big Lou slid him the rest of the cash he owed. Then, Cool gave Star the keys to the suites so they could go ahead and make themselves comfortable, while they parked the cars properly out the tow zones they were in.

"Damn Big! You look fuuuck'd up! An' Carol was just gigglin' an' shit on her way to the room!" Cool noticed.

"This niggah wanna borrow ya girl car," Big Lou said slumberly.

"Yuh, C baby," Ouija added.

"Ah'ight kinfolk," Cool grinned, as he continued. "I ain't got no problem wit' it, jus' don't tear it up niggah," he emphasized.

"It's all gravy C baby. I'ma be at the Alamo Big-Baby, if y'all need me jus' holla," Ouija replied dependably as he sped off.

"That niggah a damn fool, huh?" Cool chuckled, as he strolled toward the hotel entrance.

"Hol up dawg! I need to get my supplies out the car!" Big Lou shouted; grasping Cool's attention.

"What supplies niggah?!" Cool grimaced. "Them hoes keep condoms kinfolk!"

"I ain't talkin'-'bout that," Big Lou smirked, "I need my medicine, unda-stan'-me?"

He fetched a two-liter bottle of discolored Sprite, a Styrofoam cup, and the foil paper wrapped fry sticks out the ashtray.

"So you be drankin' that syrup shit too, huh?" Cool smirked. "I ain't gon' ask what's in the foil paper, 'cause that's discernible."

"Man, you done bumped yo head," Big Lou chuckled. "That's discernible," he mocked.

"Naw niggah," Cool smiled, "don't hate, 'cause I know how to use proper English." As they strolled inside the hotel, they got on the elevator smuggling the illicit narcotics; almost to their destination. "By the way what the hell is the Alamo?"Cool continued with curiosity.

"One of my traps," Big Lou explained. "It's a motel off of O.S.T. owned by some chinks… I use to live there once upon a time, I pump that bitch up, so my brother-in-laws there now providing for the needy, know-wha'-I'm-talkin'-'bout?"

"Dig that," Cool grinned.

"That niggah Ouija stay there too, he keep the big eye on thangs for me. I break bread with the chinks so they don't sweat me."

"Yuh, I know they don't, money hungry fuckas wors' than us." Cool quipped, as they laughed boisterously down the hallway.

Just as they were about to knock on the door, it swung open.

"I knew it was you daddy," Star began jovially, "I recognize ya voice."

"Yuh!" Carol added. "We could hear y'all all the way down the hall! What's so damn funny?!"

"Little inside jokes baby!" Big Lou began. "Ya miss me?"

"Yuh big daddy, come here!" Carol persuaded. "I see ya brought the drank," she continued; grabbing the cup out of his hand.

"Well, whattaya know!" Cool chuckled. "Big, you done created a monster!"

"What's that lean?!" Juicy gleamed.

"Oh, we mus' be feelin' better now, huh?!" Cool bantered, as they all chuckled.

"Yes daddy," Juicy replied with glee. "I want some."

"Hell yuh," Star included. "I might as well sip too!"

"Shiiid!" Big Lou leered at them. "I shouda brought an extra pint... I done fuck'd around an stepped in a room full of lean heads!" Laughing hysteria pervaded throughout the suite, at his remark.

"Well, y'all have at it," Cool sighed, "I go see my parole officer tomorrow..."

"You got some trees too cuz?" Star interrupted yearningly.

"Somethin' like that," Big Lou sneered; manifesting the fry sticks then fired one up. He then took a couple of drags and passed it to Carol.

"Ooh, that's that coo-coo!" Star enthused. "I normally don't do dip, but fuck it! Let me hit that shit Carol!" she quirked. "Don't worry daddy, we'll have your share, we can't let them white folk lock ya back up, know-wha'-I'm-talkin'-'bout?" she mimicked jokingly; causing them all to roar with laughter.

"Awww, you too kind," Cool jeered, "I'm intoxicated enough anyway, besides, I ain't tryna deteriorate my brain."

"Look whose talkin'!" Big Lou blurted. "You used to get wet up niggah! Hell, you got me started!"

Everyone chuckled, while relishing the synergism from both substances. Cool looked on shaking his head in ridicule.

"Yuh niggah, I used to get down, but that was back in high school, know-wha'-I'm-talkin'-'bout?" he retorted, as he continued. "I ain't mad at y'all though. Do the drugs, don't let'em do you."

"Coolly, baby, we jus' havin' fun," Big Lou impeded, "you don't have to lecture, usin' them o' fly ass phrases."

Since the drugs were taking a hallucinatory effect on all of their brains, they could not laugh anymore.

Star licked and whispered how horny she was in Cool's ear. This was the cue he had been anticipating. Then, Star and Juicy commence to divest his attire as he kicked back on the bed.

"Hol' up!" Big Lou stared at the scene with lust in his eyes.

"Now that's what I'm talkin'-'bout. Baby let's dip to our room," he said; holding his hand out to Carol; guiding her to the adjoining room.

"Gon' in there big daddy," Carol halted, "I need to rap wit' Cool 'bout somthin; I'll be there ina minute. He frowned perplexed, but nevertheless, did as he was told. "Cool!" she bellowed out interveningly.

"Bitch!" Star counteracted. "Don't be interrupting us?!"

Juicy giggled as she observed.

"Hoes, I ain't gon' take him!" Carol retorted, with a chuckle. "We jus' need to discuss somthin'!"

"Hurry up daddy, my pussy percolatin'! Shit!" Star bellowed in a spasmodic frenzy.

"What's up Carol baby?" Cool began. "Make it quick."

"You somethin' else," Carol smirked, shaking her head. "I jus' wanted to know who payin' fo this?"

"Ya know, I figured that's whatcha wanted," Cool hypothesized.

"Well, ya' know, a ho gotta get paid for her services," Carol uttered, in a comical way.

"I admire a concise broad, you keepin' it real. Though trickin' ain't my category, I'm willin' to pay for what I want, an' what I want, is for my kinfolk to have a good time," Cool assured.

"I don't think you a trick baby. I'm jus' tryna pay the bills... I mean, it ain't like I know dude," Carol replied sincerely.

"Dig that," Cool agreed, "give me a price."

"Jus' a C-note baby, ya see... I ain't that expensive," she disclosed meekly.

He vowed to straighten her out before they split; being he didn't have his pants on. Which, was where a small portion of his cash was.

Meanwhile, Big Lou was smoking a fry stick in the other room butt naked awaiting his sexual treat. Two minutes later Carol sashayed through the door with an affable look in her eyes. Seductively divesting her attire.

"Damn baby! I thought I was gon' have to jack off!" Big Lou joked, as they both chuckled.

"Baby," Carol tersely stated, "I was askin' 'bout my fee for service."

"Aw baby," Big Lou chuckled, "you ain't have to worry 'bout that, know-wha'-I'm-talkin'-'bout?"

They both chuckled, as she suddenly transformed. She gently kissed his thigh; causing his dick to throb in anticipation. Then she stroked his now stiff rod a couple of times, before inserting it between her luscious lips. As she bobbed her head up and down slowly on his shaft, the blissful feeling made him put down the fry-stick, and focus on the copulating that was about to go down.

When Cool strolled back in view of his vixens, he wasn't surprised to see them both devouring each other's cunts in a 69 position. His dick pulsated in his silk boxers – which was the only piece of garment on his body. While disrobing, his thoughts drifted to Angel. He started to feel a little guilty for gallivanting around. However, blithely joined in; considering how he warned Angel initially about his womanizing ways.

"We decided to start without you daddy," Star murmured; looking up at him with juices glistening around her mouth from Juicy's pussy. "I betcha that ho wanted some money, huh?" she continued on curiously.

"Fuck it! She 'bout her chips, ain't nothin' wrong wit that," Cool stressed. "Now, y'all continue what y'all was doin', shit!" The girls chuckled at his eagerness. "Where the rubbahs at? I wanna hit doggy-style, know-wha'-I'm-talkin'-'bout?" They chuckled again, as they switched their positions, in order to please him. "Yeeeah, that's what I'm talkin'-'bout," he beamed.

"Look in my purse daddy, hurry up come ram me," Star cooed, as Juicy chuckled; until she felt the slither of her girlfriend's tongue invading her snatch.

Star had her ass hiked upward – on her knees like a dog in heat – simultaneously, tongue lashing Juicy's clitoris. Between the frantic moaning and groaning; coming from Juicy's ecstasy, and the sight of Star's shaved and meaty vulva; from the rear, Cool damn near was about to shoot his load before he entered. Managing somehow to hold on, he rolled on a condom and pierced Star's sex hole fiercely; until she neglected her pussy eating duties; shivering with sheer pleasure. He pleased them both so well that they were enthralled by his energetic nature.

Chapter - 16

Morning arrived waking Cool up first, as the sun beamed through the translucent drapes. He noticed his endurance was still at its peak. The physical workouts in the joint must have really paid off, he thought. He glanced over at his soporific broads with the sneer of a stud, before he got out the bed and put his underwear on. He stood in the mirror, like Goldie in the movie, "The Mack". Envisioning the taffeta type of threads he would flaunt; mimicking the actor to the tee.

After he finished his narcissistic imagery, he decided to be intrusive, and look in on his cousin. As he snuck in the adjoining room, he slightly snickered. Big Lou was snoring boisterously, while Carol had the pillow over her head.

"Big," Cool whispered; pulling his cousin's arm; trying not to disturb Carol. "Rise an' shine, its pimpin' time," he mumbled jokingly, smiling at the droopy look in his cousin's eyes.

"What time is it?" Big Lou yawned.

"It's early kinfolk, but you know me. I'm tryna catch the worm, know-wha'-I'm-talkin'-'bout?" Cool quipped.

Big Lou glanced at the clock on the end table, and noticed it was only 8:00 a.m.

"Ain't nothin' jumpin' playa, might as well calm ya nerves, people still sleep," Big Lou smirked, as he rolled over. "Ya know that silly ass girl been beepin me all night long?"

Cool chuckled knowing it was his cousin's insane baby mother. "So niggah, ya ain't call her back?"

Carol rolled over half sleep, revealing her bare voluptuous ass, as Big Lou sat up in the bed. Grabbing a quick peep before she covered back up, Cool noticed a few dimples in her buns.

"I can handle mine playboy, you worried 'bout the wrong thang." Big Lou shot back.

"Yuh whaatevah," Cool chuckled. "I'ma bounce, you can chill if you want Big Sexy," he joked with a pansy demeanor.

Carol let out a low laugh, amused by Cool's comedy. "Y'all crazy," she interjected, as she rolled over yawning.

After Cool got dressed, he told his girls to check out before they leave, said his goodbyes, and then headed to his mom's house to change in to some less expensive attire. He was scheduled to see his parole officer, and didn't want to provoke the suspicion of partaking in any illegal tax-free activities. He knew his parole officer was a woman, because the protocol they mailed to his mom's house indicated so. Something he preferred, since he was a man with the aptitude to charm the female gender.

CS

The neighborhood looked like a ghost town – expect for the appearance of an occasional dope fiend. As Cool parked in his mom's driveway, he noticed a female crack head approaching. He stopped her in her tracks, before she tried to present the lame game they so often played.

As Cool entered the house, he tried not to disturb the sleepy heads. He then slipped on a comfortable cotton Nike warm-up, with sneakers to match. Cheap out dated apparel that fit the occasion, he thought. He sprayed on some cologne, then headed out on his way toward Telephone Road – the location of the parole office.

Almost to his destination, his pager went off. He had a gut feeling it was Angel – and his hunch was right.

"Dr. Mosley's office. May I help you?" Angel greeted cordially, through Cool's cell phone.

"What's up kinfolk?" Cool responded knowingly.

"Hey. What happen to you las'night niggah?" she asked; feigning upset.

"I got tied down," he chuckled. "Don't tell me ya miss me?"

"I do miss you baby," she uttered sincerely, "an' I'ma kick yo butt for lettin' me sleep alone... probably been whorin' aroun', huh?"

"Don't say I didn't warn ya," he joked earnestly.

"I talk to my friend 'bout the house," she evaded his retort. "He said he got something for me."

"So when can we go look at it?" he enthused. "I'm at the parole office now, I shouldn't be too long. Let's do it at lunch time."

"Alrighty. I can take an extra hour for lunch, since it's slow... You can come pick me up at twelve."

"Dig that. Ina minute then baby girl"

"Alright pooh-pooh. Bye bye."

They both hung up.

Once Cool parked, he placed his phone and pager under the seat, before walking across the street to the store. He needed to attain a ten dollar money order for his monthly supervision fees. He then, entered the filled to capacity office lounge, signed the list, and gave the receptionist his money order.

Apparently, his parole officer didn't have many clients, because she emerged out the back and called his name instantly. He never imagined her to be so tall, slender, and attractive. After they greeted each other, he followed her to the back where she shared an office with a co-worker.

"Have a seat Mr. Hudson," the parole officer began; browsing through his file on her desk. Her co-worker dispersed leaving them alone in the cubicle like office. "I see you have no stipulations. Are you employed yet?"

"Yes ma'am," Cool fabricated.

"You don't have to call me ma'am, make me sound old," she assured with a smile. Not only was she a black beauty, her demeanor appeared to be down to earth; another plus, he thought. "Tonya is my first name; you can use that or Ms. Wells... If you have a job, I need to see a check stub every month, to keep record of it."

He grinned at how amiable her character was. It was obvious she was fraternizing with him. He took it as an opportunity to mutually respond; without being disrespectful.

"Okay Tonya," he began, "I'll bring you a check stub on our next visit." He knew his homie Black would cover for him, since he owned his business. "You know if I'm gonna call you by your firs' name, I expect you to do the same."

She displayed a warm smile. "Okay then Carlos. I have a question. What kind of cologne are you wearing? Whatever it is, it sure smells good," she complimented.

"It's Cartier'. Since you're bein' so courteous, I would like to say somethin', I deem rather pleasant. I never pictured

- 182 -

you bein' so tall, appealin', an' nice," he flattered in cajoling fashion.

"Why thank you," she beamed. "So, what you thought, I was going to look like an old hag?"

"No, not at all," he expressed innocuously. "Besides, the real beauty is on the inside anyway, and I can tell you possess such beauty."

"That is the nicest thing someone has said to me ina long time," she uttered; candidly leering in his eyes. "I need more clients like you."

"An' I'm sure the system need mo' warm hearted parole officers like yourself," he charmed continuously.

"My. Your words are so soothing," she smiled, as she began to prowl. "I bet all your girlfriends, simply adore you."

Cool chuckled; knowing his eloquence was working. "I noticed you put emphasis on the girlfriend part of your statement," he teased.

"Not really... it's jus'... well, since you're so much of a gentleman, I'm just merely assuming you have more than one girl, that's all," she replied with a veneer innocence. He let out a low laugh. "What's so funny?!" she chuckled. "I'm serious!"

"Nothin'," he down played, as he continued. "Never mind me... It's jus' that, I see mo' good qualities in you. We jus' met, an' you can see the secrets within my soul. I'll admit, I have a ravenous appetite for females, but I try to treat them all like ladies."

"I see," she chuckled. "Well, I'm not going to hold you up. You seem intellectual enough to have business to tend to. I must say it was rather interesting meeting you. Let me walk you out." She stood up, as he followed suit. "One more matter, though. My supervisor require me to do a urinalysis every other month on my no risk clients."

"That's not a problem. I drink sporatically, hopefully you won't violate me fo that, huh?"

"I have no problem with you drinking, as long as you don't catch a case doing so."

They left the office and idly strolled toward the lobby. Since their conversation was so intriguing, Cool decided to subtly coax her out on a luncheon date. Just to see her response.

"Ya know, I hope I'm not over steppin' my boundaries," Cool began, breaking the silence. "But if I don't ask, I have this strange felling I might regret it later. Anyway, we need to do lunch one day soon."

"Well, I'm not really allowed to get involved with my clients," Tonya dejected. "But I just might take you up on that offer... What they don't know, won't hurt them, right?" she mumbled.

"I agree," he replied cheerfully; elated by her decision. "So, I guess it's cool for me to give you my digits then?"

"Sure. Here's some paper and a pen." He wrote his pager number down, excited about his progress. "I'll give you a call, take care," she coquetted as she sashayed away.

"You too," he replied, before strutting out the building with the aura of a pimp.

Chapter - 17

W hen Cool phoned Black to fill him in about the house, he eagerly wanted to ride with them to go check it out. Since Cool was only fifteen minutes from his house, it didn't take him long to get there, pick him up, and be enroute toward Angel's workplace.

"So, where the crib at? Ya know we don't need it 'round the wrong niggahs?" Black said, as they cruised down the street almost to their destination.

"Already. It's on the southwest ... I think Mo city" Cool contemplated, as he continued. "That's why I picked you up, so you can help give the approval niggah."

"So, what you an' Money get off into las'night?"

"I was gettin my freak on. I ain't fuck wit' Money las'night, when I called him, he was gettin' his serve on… Oh yuh, don't let me forget to give you some of that loot I accumulated."

"You better stop ridin' 'round wit' that shit! Be lookin' like dick face if them po-pos pull you over an' take it!" they both chuckled at Black's paradoxical statement.

"You sure right. I was gon' let Angel hol' it, but I might as well break you off?"

"Dig that. So you an' Angel done got real chummy, huh?" Black teased.

"We ah'ight," Cool down played.

"Niggah! I bet you hit it! You think you slick, huh?!" They both roared with laughter, as Black continued. "Ain't nothin' to be shame about damn fool! She cool peeps!"

They were now pulling in the parking lot at the doctor's office. Cool spotted Angel's vehicle and parked next to it.

"I ain't trippin' kinfolk. But, I ain't tryna let nothin' intervene in my panderin' scheme. Feel me? Let me shoot in here an' get this girl." Cool explained before getting out the car.

When Cool strolled inside the doctor's office, Angel was on the computer finishing up some sort of undertaking; assuring him she would be ready in ten minutes. After greeting all of her co-workers, he informed Angel he would be waiting for her in the car.

After Angel phoned the realtor to get the directions, she clocked out and went outside browsing around for the car. Cool blew the horn getting her attention. Black allowed her to sit in the front seat, as they greeted each other mutually.

"Hey pooh-pooh," Angel said, as she leaned over giving Cool a kiss.

"What's goin' down? You ain't ate yet, huh?" Cool asked, as Black grinned in the backseat; knowing he assumed right.

"Naw. I could go for a salad," Angel responded.

"Well, I'm hungry," Black interjected, "I ain't ate shit this mornin'."

"We can go get somethin', after we finish the crib business," Cool suggested, "I wanna try out that Pappasito's place… I heard they got good Mexican food."

"I'm down with it," Black added.

"I don't care either.... I know one thing, you sure like that Mexican food. Let me find out you got a little Spanish in your blood," Angel replied jokingly, as they all chuckled at her comment.

"Stop at that liquor sto' dawg!" Black suddenly announced, as he pointed in the direction.

"Where fool?" Cool gestured.

"To your left, in that strip center over there by that Stop-N-Go. My foreign homie be hookin' me up," Black explained.

As Cool whipped in the strip center, the liquor store his homie spoke of came into view. They both hopped out to purchase a bottle leaving Angel in the car.

"What's happening fellas?" the owner of the liquor store greeted, as they entered.

"Wha'd up mane?" Black replied. "This here is my homie Cool."

"What's happening Cool? Nice to meet you, my name's Rod," the owner held out his hand, giving him a firm handshake.

Cool obliged his acquaintance.

"So, what you do me a Remy Martin XO for?" Black interjected.

"For you. The usual ten percent off, you know that," Rod smirked.

He then took the bottle off the shelf, complimenting them on their fine taste in liquor.

As they exited the store, Black grabbed a bag of chips near the entrance. Rod didn't mind giving away small freebies to the customers that came in squandering C-notes.

"Before you pull off, fix us a drank," Black asked with courtesy. "You want some chips Angel?"

"No thankya," Angel replied.

Cool poured both cups to the rim. Handing his comrade one, while placing the other one in his cup holder.

"Pass the chips niggah! Greedy ass tryna eat 'em all up!" he sneered comically.

"Here ya go kinfolk," Black grumbled, "a niggah hungry goddamn-me."

"I'm hungry too niggah! Bad enough ya got me drankin' this shit ona empty stomach!"

"Aw, quit cryin wimp. You'll be ah'ight," Black uttered sarcastically.

They arrived in a timely fashion. Angel cracked up off of their antics, as she observed how giddy they were from their first sip of alcohol.

"Damn! I'm fuck'd up already!" Cool announced, as they all chuckled. He then displayed an askance look at an approaching vehicle. "Looks like your friend here baby girl," he uttered, as the others observed as well.

"That's him," Angel assured.

The shady featured, but well groomed man got out of his car and proceeded in their direction.

"This niggah looks like a crooked car salesman," Cool joked.

Their hoopla caused the realtor to display a warm smile, as he also grew self-conscious.

"What's so amusing? I could use a good laugh myself," the realtor responded curiously.

"Nothin', jus' a little inside joke," Angel clarified. She introduced him to Black and Cool.

They all cordially shook hands, then strolled toward the entrance of the house. Since the neighborhood looked tranquil enough, and the house befitted their criteria, they all deemed it was time to discuss the down payment, as well as the monthly rent.

"So, Bill. How much is it gon' cost us to move in?" Angel proceeded on.

"Well," Bill began, "it's seven-fifty a month. You have to pay first and last months rent, and a twenty dollar application fee. It's my personal place so I'll waive the deposit."

"Soun' good to me," Cool blurted. "Whatcha think Black?"

"Let's do it," Black concurred.

"Get me a money order today, and Angel, I need you to fill out the application for me…" the realtor paused, as he handed her a contract from his briefcase. It only took her ten minutes to review, fill it out, and sign it. "Okay, it's settled. Once I get the money order, you all can get the keys and move in A.S.A.P…. Usually I run background checks on my clients, but Angel's my girl," he smiled; assuring them of how fortunate they were to have Angel on their team.

"Well, hell, I know where a post office is nearby. Let's shoot over there right quick," Cool suggested vigorously toward Black. "Hol' it down Angel, we'll be right back. Ah'ight?"

"Okay baby," Angel replied nonchalantly.

The post office was only fifteen minutes away. They were back in no time. Since the proceedings went down so quickly, Bill gave them the keys, vowing to send someone by to tidy up a bit.

"Here's some of my business cards gentlemen. If you all run into anyone who's looking to buy, rent, or even sell a house, give me call," Bill said shaking everyone's hand, before leaving the scene.

While Angel further inspected the house, the homies decided to wait on her in the car. They sipped on their cognacs, while discussing issues.

"Now, all we need is Jerry's partner to come put us a tight stash spot in the crib," Black suggested.

"Already," Cool began, "I'm really ready to get my grind on now."

"Now that we got the crib, I'ma start gettin' them fi'ty birds fat ass been tryna lay on me," Black proclaimed.

"Already!" Cool responded, as he turned toward the backseat; giving his homie some dap in agreement. "It ain't finna be nothing nice... Ya boy got big plans that's gon' bring along a lot of overhead… but will pay off in the long run. Ya-hear-me?"

Angel appeared abruptly. As she got in the car, their discussion came to a halt.

"Well, pooh-pooh, looks like I'ma need some money," she requested, as Cool leered towards her.

"No pun intended baby girl," Cool sighed. "But what the hell ya need money for? "

"Get off the ends big daddy!" Black intervened.

"Fuck you o'black ass niggah!" Cool retorted, causing them all to chuckle.

"It's for the house pooh-pooh, I guess you can say it's for me indirectly," Angel replied, as she leaned toward the backseat. "Leave my pooh alone Black!"

"Ah'ight, I'll let your pooh bear make it, for now," Black bantered, as they all chuckled. "I'll contribute a little somethin' to the crib too, " he assured.

"Shit, we gon' need e'erythang... I'll give ya somethin' to work wit' baby girl," Cool asserted. "So whatcha got on it Black?"

"Niggah, I'll give ya a thee! I ain't gon' be livin' there, so don't expect too much," Black shot back .

"That's chill, I ain't trippin', jus' give it to Angel... I know you got it kinfolk," Cool chuckled.

They were now pulling in the parking lot of Pappasito's. A nice Mexican restaurant that was not too far from Angel's workplace.

After they finished eating their scrumptious meals – between the both of them – they gave her four thousand dollars to buy some necessities for the house. Then, they cruised back to her job to drop her off.

CS

When the hotel maids entered the suite to tidy up for the next guest, they had no idea there were people still inside asleep. The Spanish dialect startled Juicy, as the working women barged in to do their chores.

"Pardon senorita. I'll clean later," one of the maids expressed courteously.

"Thank you ma'am! Ya scared me!" Juicy sighed; clutching her chest. The Spanish women back pedaled out the suite with their cleaning cart; smiling displaying gold grills, as they proceeded on to the next suite. Their mouths reminded Juicy of the ghetto fabulous way some black folks like to embellish their teeth, with the precious metal. As she yawned, she glanced at the clock realizing it was an hour past check out time. "Star!" she bellowed out to no avail.

She then, smacked Star on her bare ass; definitely getting her attention now.

"Damn bitch!" Star yelped with a frown, as she rolled over.

"It's time to go ho!" Juicy chuckled with cadence. "It's way pass check out time girl!"

"What time is it?" Star yawned.

"One o'clock, an' hour pass check out time!" Juicy responded animatedly. "Let me go over here an' wake Carol tired ass up too!"

"Damn!" Star flustered. "I don't feel like movin'. Shit!"

Star turned over and buried her face in the pillow, while Juicy strolled over to the other room to give Carol a rude awakening.

The girls all washed up before putting on their apparel. Then, they all sashayed down to the front desk to checkout, causing commotion along the way. They didn't care if people were disturbed, especially since they proudly represented the risque´ and rambunctious.

Some of the lounging ofays despised the girls, while other ones adored their out spoken appeal. One of the horny caucasians from out of town, build up the courage to flirt with Star when they were leaving the front desk. Which was right up her alley to add another trick to her roster. Especially a white older one. She knew they paid well, and were easier to please.

"Hi honey," the stranger began upon his approach.

"Hey baby," Star coquetted, as the other girls looked on curiously.

The natty gentleman continued conversing concisely. "I'm here on business, and I was wondering if you would like to join me for cocktails... or something later on," he grinned deviously; scrutinizing her from head to toe.

"I have to work later on, but..." she was cut off, by his intense desire to know.

"What do you do for a living," he uttered intrusively.

"I'm an exotic dancer, if you make it worth my while baby, perhaps I could come back, an' show you some of my moves," Star uttered seductively.

"Yes siree," he chuckled, leering at her alluring bodily assets. "Why don't you show back here around seven o'clock, at the bar, and we'll discuss the details."

"Tell you what baby," Star began; pulling a business card out of her purse. "Page me if you serious" she said before wiggling her ass away; purposefully knowing he would be watching.

She feigned like her time was being wasted, just to see his reaction.

"I guess I need to page you before seven o'clock then!" he said loud enough for her to hear in the short distance.

She looked over her shoulder winking her eye, as she and her counterpart's sauntered out of the hotel.

CS

Driving along on their way to drop off Carol, they continued carrying on with the energy of brazen women. Socially criticizing, being messy, and so forth. A ritual that personified all young women of their calibers.

"Well, ho's, looks like I got me a date for later on," Star snickered, as they rode along to their destination.

"Let me know if you need some help bitch! I need to make me some mo' cho-chos!" Carol added with a chuckle.

"Girl, I donno if I should go home," Juicy distressed; altering their jolly mood with her skepticism. "Tank gon' probably try to kill me!"

"Don't worry 'bout that baby… I gotcha back," Star assured; running her fingers through Juicy's hair.

"Y'all some freaky ho's," Carol quipped, as they all chuckled. "Y'all shoulda let that loco ass niggah… What's his name?"

"Ouija bitch," Juicy heckled.

"Anyway, y'all shoulda took his ass over there wit' y'all… You know that name remind me of somethin'," Carol grimaced in doubt.

"The spirit game scatter brain," Star barbed.

Carol shot her the middle finger, as they chuckled.

They were now back at the club dropping Carol off to her car; which didn't appear to be vandalized. A blessing considering the crime rate in that area.

"Well, I see you ho's later. Y'all comin to work?" Carol said getting out the car.

"Damn right!" Star emphasized. "We gotta make our cho-chos jus' like you bitch! Besides, we want daddy to be proud of us… Okay?!" she stressed; giving Juicy dap.

"See!" Carol cackled. "That fly ass niggah put that whip appeal on you ho's."

"Call it what you want," Juicy interjected, "we got business to tend to, so we'll see your tired ass later."

"Excuse me," Carol smirked. "Bye bitches!" she said, as they watched her twist away like a ho on the stroll.

As they continued their journey to Juicy's place, silently bobbing their head to an explicit Too Short rap tape; a noise jutted out the glove compartment.

"What's that girl?" Star asked curiously.

"Sounds like my pager girl, hand it to me please, it's in the glove box," Juicy replied.

"That's cute," Star smiled, as she fetch the pager, "soun' like a Christmas carol or somethin'."

She scanned the pager noticing by the familiar code that it was her baby daddy. At least he wasn't calling from the apartment, she thought.

"Guess who this is girl," Juicy announced disgusted.

"The way you look it mus' be Tank," Star chuckled. "Is he at your place?"

"Naw. But I kno it's him... I can tell by his code... You got your phone on you girl?"

"Yuh, it's in my purse." She searched her purse for a few seconds. "Here ya go."

"Thank ya baby," Juicy sighed, as she dialed the number, then greeted him with a pompous attitude. "Hello,"

"Hello. This Juicy?" Tank asked; sounding more subdued than his normal belligerent self.

"This she. What's up?" she replied callously; finally realizing she was apart of a family that would guard her from harm.

"Baby," Tank continued remorsefully, "I been thinkin', an' I know I been treatin' you like shit... Ya listenin' baby?"

Her mind was made up. She knew what he was about to say, but wanted to hear him beg anyway "I'm here," she sighed arrogantly.

"Well, I want us to start over... ya know... be a family again. Maybe the pistol whippin' did me some good. I know you jus' be tryna get paid... I had no business tryna hit on you anyway, so ba..." she cut him off.

"Tank what you want faded a long time ago. Opportunity knocked, so I'm takin' advantage of it. We can be friends, 'cause we got a child together, otha than that... It's over," she resolved.

"So, it's like that, huh? I tol' you I was sorry! At leas' you can give me anotha chance!" he pleaded.

"What!" she sneered. "I can't believe you goin' there wit' me. Ya know you a trip! Tell ya what, when you want to see our baby, I'll make arrangements. I'm at the apartment now gettin' my. . ." he cut her off.

"You there now? Stay there baby, I'm coming through, we need to talk."

"You don't need to come through, till after I leave! I jus' need to get my clothes, you can have everything else."

She was now driving through the security gate of her apartment. While Star observed, commending her on the way she was handling Tank.

"I guess you got yo' new niggah wit'cha, huh?" Tank scoffed.

"Whaatevah! The lease will be up next month, on my way out I'm lettin' the manager know I'm not renewin' it."

"You serious, huh?"

"What you think this a game?! Look... I gotta go."

"Well, fuck you then bitch!"

"Jus' what I thought, you'll never change."

"Wait. I..."

She hung up in his face.

The girls went inside and collected all of Juicy's worthy possessions. Then, they loaded the car to capacity, while managing to make room for themselves. Afterwards, they left in a hurry, just in case Tank decided to show up.

As they cruised along, Juicy phoned her mom, to merely fill her in on the scenario; just in case Tank spitefully nabbed their baby, and abscond incommunicado.

"Ya know, I'm glad Cool came along girl, I needed to really diss Tank tired ass a long time ago," Juicy stressed, after she hung up with her mom.

"Okay?! Cool gon' be our knight in shinin' armor girl," Star concurred, as they both chuckled.

"I don't even feel bad about what I'm doin' girl."

"Me too girl.... A bitch need guidance anyway. I don't mine givin' my cho-chos to somebody that's gon' make good use of 'em."

"Sure ya right, 'cause Tank sorry ass ain't know what to do wit' money, but fuck it off."

"Okay?! I'ma call Carl so we can look at some houses. I'm ready to get this thang started girl."

"It's gon' be all good baby."

"I know. I believe in Cool, he not gon' let us down. Watch girl! We gon' have it goin' on!" Star bragged.

"I believe in him too," Juicy conceded.

"See?! That niggah got us both sprung!"

They both chuckled, giving each other dap.

"Yuh, he fly… Don't I take this exit girl?"

"Yuh, get off here, I live in the complex to the left." Star detailed.

"I see'em," Juicy observed in the distance.

"I need to page that bitch Porsche, an' let her know what time it is."

"Yeah. She still like tootin' that shit girl?" Juicy asked curiously.

"Hell yes. She ain't gon' never stop doin' that shit," Star grimaced.

They chuckled knowingly.

"So you gon' tell daddy 'bout her problem?"

"Naw, I ain't gon' do her like that. Between me an' you, I toot a little bit… I don't have no problem wit' it like Porsche do, though."

"Girl I didn't know you fuck aroun' too. Don't worry, your secret safe wit' me baby."

"Thanks baby. I don't want daddy to think I'ma cokehead…. Come on let's get this shit out the car, we got otha engagements. I want my daddy to be proud of me, when I dump a shit load of cho-chos in his lap."

They got out the car cackling, as they gathered some of the load, and headed toward the apartment. Ironically, when Star opened the door, they could hear snoring in the distance.

"Who's that on your couch girl?" Juicy muttered, as Star strolled toward the covered up human lump.

"Bitch!" Star responded; popping her target directly on the buttocks. "How you get in here ho?"

"Shit you wasn't here," Porsche yawned, as she looked up, "so I came through the window."

Star shook her head in ridicule, as they all chuckled.

"Let me go get anotha load," Juicy announced, before she headed back to the car.

"Get anotha load," Porsche grimaced. "What the hell goin' on?"

"She movin' in wit' me," Star declared with glee.

"I'll say," Porsche smirked. "So that's who you been wit' all night, huh?"

"Naw bitch," Star chuckled; recognizing her insinuation. "We been wit' our daddy all night."

"Y'all daddy! What the fuck?! Don't tell me you done hooked back up wit' ...." Star cut her off.

"Hell naw! My new daddy way mo' thorough, know-wha'-I'm-sayin?" Star assured.

"Hm," Porsche smirked. "Niggah mus' be like that. You done gave the niggah the title of nobility already."

They both chuckled, giving each other dap.

I know girl, his witty ways won me," Star confessed. "You know him too, you met him at his comin' home party the otha day."

"Who bitch?!"

"Cool, Black homeboy."

"Oh, so he the niggah got you so happy-go-lucky?"

"Anyway... Bitch we formin' a family. You gon' be down or what?"

"Ho you know I'm wit it."

Juicy reappeared with some more of her clothes, while Star continued explaining the details. They were mutually atturned to the way they were willing to put in work for their newly throned dictator.

Cool's chicanery on the girls worked well. Now, he needed to stay focused to excel to a more prestigious level. Embodying his ventures; insuring the best of both worlds. A legitimate and illicit way of life; something he envisioned while incarcerated.

GLOSSARY

Ace Boon Coon: Close friend, associate, or partner.

Ballin': Extravagant spending

Ball til you fall: Extravagant splurge, that come to a halt when something terrible happens.

Barn yard pimp: Chicken.

Bounce: To leave.

Blunt: Cigar filled with mariguana.

Brick/Bird: Kilo of Cocaine.

Bucket/Hooptie: An old automobile that barely run.

Cadillac Gig: A laid back job that do not require much physical labor.

Cheeba/Trees: Mariguana.

Chips /Cho-Chos/Scrilla/Piece of Change/Ends: Money.

CO: Correctional Officer.

Cracka: Caucasian person or white person.

Crisp and Clean: Well groom attire.

Dap: Hand slap greeting.

Diss: Disregard.

Dizzam: Damn.

Five-O: Po-Po,Police.

Fly: Smooth, cunning, dapper.

Fry Sticks/Dip: Weed joint lace with PCP.

G (Gangsta): A person with a vast amount of street knowledge; from years of experience.

G'd Up: Dressed in the latest fashion.

Grill: Fancy precious metal teeth.

Hit the Bricks: Free from incarceration.

Hit a lick/Stang: Make some money.

Homie/Homeboy: Close friend, associate, partner, or pal.

Hood Rat/ Boppa/ Skeezer/ Hoochie: A party type women down for any occasion.

It's all gravy: It's all good.

Kite: Letter.

Koolaid: Cool

Lean/Syrup: Cough syrup with codeine ingredients.

Out of Pocket: Not around.

Reggie: Regular Mariguana.

Shooting the shit/Choppin' it up: Idle talk.

Skeezed: Have sex.

Slab: A tricked out automobile; usually an older model.(slow, loud, and bangin)

Spread: Jail house feast.

Spread the Hustle: To hustle more ways than one.

Stole On: Hit with a punch unknowingly.

Rack Time: Jail house bedtime.

Rank on/Dirty Dozens: To bad mouth someone in a joking manner.

Ponderosa/Crib: Place of residence.

Player Hater: A person envious of another person success.

Props: Recognition.

Pull your coat: To inform a person of news, events, happenings, etc.

T-Jones: Mom/Mother.

Thee: A Thousand.

Trap: A place where drugs are sold.

Tube: TV.

Wet up: High on fry sticks.

Underground Juggling: Illegitimate hustling.

Zydot: A pill that cleanse the body system.

Calvin Haynes

About the Author

Calvin Haynes was born and raised in Houston, Texas. After his early years at Sterling High School, he attended computer courses at a Community College. During the course of his education and some very turbulent isolated years, Calvin discovered his passion for writing. Calvin was inspired with his creative thinking skills when his friends would approach him with their girlfriend problems. He would then take the liberty to write compassionate letters on behalf of his friends to give to their beloved frustrated disheartened mates. Once the letters were read, Voila! It was intriguing to Calvin, because the letters illustrated a faux intellectual side to his friends that their girlfriends were truly unaware of. The secret they didn't know was that Calvin was behind the mastered set of orchestrated words that was to restore the strength of their once broken union. Needless to say....the letters were all a success. It was then Calvin knew he was blessed with a street work of art.

Calvin truly believes in the divine powers that be. He is the founder of Corporate Street Publications and owns multiple successful business establishments. Calvin enjoys going to the gun range, weight lifting, applying his imagination to new writing concepts and enjoying life exquisitely. He is an avid giver and believes in supporting others. Calvin still resides with his loving family in Houston, Texas. Betrayal of Peers is his first trilogy of novels.

The Betrayal Continues.....

Rewards of the Hustle
(Book II)

Pitfalls of the Hustle
(Book III)

Corporate Street Apparel

Purchase online at
www.calvinhaynes.com

Designed to Make You Think,

In order to teach yourself...

Betrayal of Peers
(Inception of the Hustle)
Purchase Form

Name_____

Address_____

City_____State_____ Zip_____

Email:_____

Qty:_____ $14.99 each

Sub Total:_____
Sales Tax:_____
Shipping:_____ $2.95 per book
Total:_____

Please make check or money order payable to:
Corporate Street Publication
PO BOX 682153
Houston, TX 77268

For online purchases go to:
www.calvinhaynes.com

Thank you for your support!

We want to hear from you. Please share with us, your comments on the read of this novel. We appreciate your feedback!

_____

_____

_____

_____

_____

_____

www.ingramcontent.com/pod-product-compliance
Lightning Source LLC
Chambersburg PA
CBHW070003260626
47159CB00005B/1648